INK STAINS

A DARK FICTION LITERARY ANTHOLOGY

INK STAINS

A DARK FICTION LITERARY ANTHOLOGY

Volume 1

Edited by
N. Apythia Morges

Dark Alley Press

INK STAINS ANTHOLOGY
Volume 1

ISBN 13: 978-0-692-62811-9
ISBN 10: 0-692-62811-8

© 2016 by Dark Alley Press
Individual stories copyright by authors
"A Grave Tale" @ Eddie Cantrell
"Eden" @ A. O'Neal
"Phoenix" @ J. S. Watts
"Pretty Little Ironies" @ Tamela J. Ritter
"The Art of Living" @ Michelle K. Bujnowski
"The Red Shawl" @ Steph Minns
"The Dark Walk" @ John McFarland
"Twice Per Annum" @ Aaron Vlek

Dark Alley Press
http://www.darkalleypress.com

An imprint of Vagabondage Press LLC
PO Box 3563
Apollo Beach, Florida 33572
http://www.vagabondagepress.com

First edition printed in the United States of America and the United Kingdom, March 2016

10 9 8 7 6 5 4 3 2 1

Front cover art by Black Blood. Cover designed by Maggie Ward.

INK STAINS

A DARK FICTION LITERARY ANTHOLOGY

TABLE OF CONTENTS

PRETTY LITTLE IRONIES

Tamela J. Ritter

She likes pretty things. He knows this. Knows it as well as he knows there is nothing about him that is pretty. Pretty isn't really a requirement he's ever needed. *Pickled Punk's Menagerie of Oddities* didn't have much use for dainty or for precious in their performers. This is why she stands out as unique. She is seven feet of silks, satins, and things he can't name that make her sparkle and shimmer. He is rough, calloused, and has entirely too much hair. He knows this too. Yet, his want for her makes him yearn for things he thought he'd never have. Most of these yearnings are for companionship, someone who understands him, who has similar experiences with the horror that is most of the human race.

There is another yearning though. To be touched by hands that have force enough to permeate past the matted fur, the top layer of tough, thick skin, to touch someone who would appreciate his roughened fingers. Someone he doesn't have to worry about breaking with the force of his need.

They take walks together, and she lets him loop his arm through hers. They share meals, and she listens with big sad eyes to his stories of cruelty and isolation. Later, when he walks her back to her tent, she allows him to kiss her good night. All the while, he waits.

After months of this leisurely courtship, she invites him to dinner in her personal space. No one has ever invited him into her home before. He breaks twelve combs preparing for the evening. She said she wanted to show him something. Something she's never shared before. He thinks this is his chance to share something of his own.

Dinner is rather a glamorous affair with candles and big, bold flowers, and she is nervous in her taffeta and pearls, her eyes mixed with anxiety and need as she giggles loudly at everything. He watches her flick her gaze to the back room from time to time, and that, along with the heady scents of meat cooking and the cut flowers dying, makes his palms sweat and his heart beat irregularly.

They are dancing after dinner. He marvels at the size of her space, that the two of them, both monsters, could sway back and forth without tearing the fabric walls down around them. His hand flat against the small of her back, he pulls her close to him, resting his head on her chest, feeling the fleshy softness and the beat of her rapidly pulsing heart. He marvels at her size all over again, that he found someone who towers over him—he'd never met anyone larger than him—and yet still smells sweet and is kind about his clumsy attempts at suaveness. He slides his hand up her back in between her shoulder blades, where he circles and massages in rough swipes that cause her breath to hitch. He wonders if it's been hard for her too, finding someone who can satisfy her giant wants and needs. He knows he can, as he moves his lips to whisper nonsense up her chest, her neck, and, finally, her ear.

She pulls back and looks scandalized, and he knows he has said too much. He has laid his desire bare, and she is horrified by it. But then, she takes his hand, pulls him gently to the back of the tent to the place where the hanging fabric walls meet, looking at him through her eyelashes, a blush faint on her cheeks. She tells him she has never trusted anyone with what she wants to show him. He swallows, nods, and follows, matching her shuffle, fighting the urge to tackle her through the door and ravish her. Before she opens it, she looks at him again, and he sees her silent plea: *Understand me! Accept me! Love me!* His heart expands painfully against his rib cage. Not forgetting that she is also a victim of cruelty, someone who has developed her rough edges to avoid pain, he sees that the look also says: *Or I will crush you with my thighs as I scoop your heart out of your chest and eat it, while you watch!* He doesn't know which part entices him more.

He stops when he sees the hazy dream of a room. His jaw drops, and his eyes flit around trying to find one thing that feels solid and familiar. It is a fruitless search. He has walked into a cloud of pouf and pastels, and he feels as if he's soiling it with his mere presence. She turns to smile at him, and he swallows his uneasiness and allows her to pull him further in. And then she's opening a door to a large wardrobe, and he's overcome all over again. Inside are row after perfect row of lifeless eyes, candied lips and rosy cheeks. There are girls in lace and silks, hair in curls and ribbons; boys in velvet knee pants, buckle shoes, ruffled shirts. The dolls are perfect and well cared for, and his whole body shivers with confused arousal and revulsion.

She is talking, but he doesn't hear what she says as she takes his hand and pulls him closer. The faces on the dolls are too lifelike; he can see in them the boys and girls who point and laugh, who scream, cry, and run from him on the midway when he dares to venture out. He finds himself holding his breath waiting to hear theirs. She reaches out and touches one of the girls, and then she is holding it and bringing it to him, and she's nervous and shy, but he sees something in her eyes that is both anxious and wanton. She brings the doll, past him to the mirrored table in the corner of the room. His nose is assaulted by rose and lavender and something that makes his hair curl. She sits the doll at the vanity and begins taking the bobby pins out of the doll's hair.

He doesn't know what possesses him to do it, but he goes up behind her and begins taking the bobby pins out of *her* hair, and she sighs, leaning into him.

"My perfect porcelain doll," he calls her, and she reaches for his hand, still at her hair, and brings it to her lips. She kisses his rough, meaty palm delicately; he moans. Then she takes each finger and kisses it wet and loud before taking his thumb, wetting it with her tongue, taking it in her mouth and sucking.

So overcome, he clutches her and tries to pull her to him. She holds her own and protectively wraps her hand around the doll before her. She tells him he must be careful and that the one thing dolls teach is that being delicate and precise is its own reward. If he were delicate with her and the things she loved, he too would be rewarded, she says. With a blush, he nods and swallows. Waiting.

Then she sits down and pulls out a large brush, which she hands to him, and a smaller brush that she begins to run through the doll's hair. Watching the care she takes, he mimics her, and her contented sigh tells him she likes it. After a while, he pulls out a chair to sit behind her, putting her long hair in one hand and bringing the brush through it over and over until the hair shines. Just when he starts to wonder where his prize is, he feels her slowly moving back and readjusting herself in between his legs. All the time, she continues to care for the doll, and he continues to primp her and massage her scalp as she gets closer. He knows this pleases her because she moans and leans into him further.

Finally she puts down her toy. She is sitting on his lap now, arm around him, but still looking at the doll. He doesn't know what to do with his hands anymore, so he wraps one around her waist and nervously places the other on her thigh, waiting to be slapped away. She doesn't even seem to notice.

"Isn't she beautiful?" she asks.

He looks at the woman on his lap, the doll all but forgotten. "The most beautiful," he whispers.

In the proceeding months, he learns the things she will allow him to do. The way she will touch him and allow him to fondle her is dependent upon where her dolls are in the room. He thinks maybe it's because she needs an audience, and he is so overcome with lust and desperation for her that he doesn't object, even if he finds it slightly unsettling as she lays the dolls around the bed. If she likes to gaze dreamily at them as she straddles him, who is he to complain? He's never been with anyone—or any*thing* for that matter—that can take all that he has to give, and if she likes to see the beautiful things surrounding her rather than him on top of her, rutting against her with snorts and grunts, who could blame her?

He also learns that she loves more than anything to receive gifts. Almost anything pleases her, but nothing more than trinkets for her dolls. Especially since he is the only one she has shared this obsession with. And he's certain it's an obsession. But who is he to judge what a person loves, especially if one of those things are him? Instead he hunts for clothes and accessories she can use for her beautiful, life-like dolls. And he realizes more and more just how life-like they are, but he tries not to think of that too much as he spends his time and a great deal of his earnings on shops online. They wrap the gifts so delicately and apply so much crepe and gauzy finery of ribbons and bows to the boxes that he would never know how to do himself. He takes the credit though, and when she points her painted finger at him and curls it in a "come here" motion, he goes to her, every time.

She shocks him with her ferocity. Watching her with the dolls as she removes one fancy dress and replaces it with another, he starts to think of her as a petite debutante. When she's put them back on their pedestals and comes to him with a nervous giggle before grabbing him tightly and throwing him on the bed, he remembers, she is anything but a delicate flower. She is a ravenous giant of a woman with wants and needs as large and wanton as his own. His rewards are many and nothing else really matters. He would do anything for her and for what she gives to him in return.

The boy is so pretty.

Very few of the children who show up and follow the caravan are. There is a certain sickness that permeates the sort of urchin who dreams of running away and joining the circus, the traveling shows. Or, maybe all children do, but it is usually the low, the malnourished, and the scarred that actually take the step and stowaway. But not this boy.

The boy snuck into one of the truck beds outside of Albuquerque. He had seen the boy run alongside, felt the dip when he jumped in and threw the tarp over himself. He hadn't said anything and later would drop some bread where the boy would find it. He was always the one who drew the children out of their hiding places once they were far enough away that they couldn't just go back. He gave them jobs, got them settled.

It was also his job to take care of them when, as happened from time to time, there were accidents. Some things are just too precious for this world.

And yes, now that the boy lies before him with lifeless eyes and a stilled heart, some of that sparkle and shimmer are gone, but there is a fragile delicacy replacing it that haunts him as he scoops the boy into his arms. He doesn't really think of the why or the explanation, he just wants to show her this beautiful boy, to share this with her. She deserves pretty things; she knows how to appreciate them. She will help him prepare the body, make the boy shine again with her caring touch.

He brings the boy to her tent and waits for the crowds of grief and hysterical agitation to die down. He knows there are things he should be doing; they will have to pack up and move again, sooner than expected. All he can think of, though, is the reward he is sure will be bestowed on him, how overcome with emotion she'll be and the allowances he'll receive. The things he used to only have vague desires for have recently become reality and are now an obsession that drowns out all right and reason.

"Ohhh, *magnifique*," she whispers through her teeth when she finally enters the tent and sees him lying there, waiting for her. "It is exquisite."

Horrified, he thinks she doesn't understand. This "it" before her isn't a doll, not like her other playthings. He was a boy; only moments before, he had breath and hope, wants, needs, strengths, and potential, so much potential. But then she's taking the boy's clothes off, reaching for a large black bag, and with a quick and precise touch, she's pulling out tubes and needles, vials, and IV bags of some sort of thick liquid. All the while, she's singing a lullaby and looking fondly at her newest toy. And with a sick thunk of realization, he knows it was he who didn't understand, had never understood. All those dolls, all those lives lost, and she wraps them in finery and glitter and calls it a hobby.

He feels the bile rise up in him. Then she looks at him, and she has that certain fire in her eyes, and he swallows the sick along with his self-loathing and comes to where she's urging him. She gets on her knees before him. He wants to refuse, to step away and deny her fumbling fingers from removing his trousers. He wants to take the boy back to where he found him, leave him for the bereft, and forget those dead eyes that will never again close, will never again stop staring at him. What he really wants, what he prays for, is for his body to not react to her urgent attentions.

He closes his eyes tight and curses as he feels the prickle of his skin when her fingernails scratch up his thighs. He hears her whisper her endearments, her pet names for him, but underneath it he swears he can hear the boy, calling out for him. *Take me to my family. Please, take me back.* He tastes salt and soil on his lips from sweat and begs his body to remain as lifeless as the boy on the bed before them. A low, guttural growl is his undoing, and he whimpers as she teases. He feels his body's betrayal. He opens his eyes and sees everything with a softened haze of the tears in his eyes. All he can do now is pray for a speedy release so that he may run away, may cleanse himself of this mess.

She holds him in her long, delicate fingers and breathes in hot whispers, as if she's talking to one of her dolls. Her corpses.

"Shuddup," he orders, and she thinks he means he needs her mouth. And in a way, he does, but not because he wants it, wants her. He wants her gone, wants all memory of her and his need of her gone.

As she wraps her mouth around him, his eyes find the boy and he pleads for mercy, absolution, or, at the least, understanding. *I didn't know*, he cries silently. *I didn't sort out what it all meant.*

This boy wouldn't know though, wouldn't understand. He imagines the boy's never wanted for anything in his life, never been denied a single thing. He wouldn't understand how hard it is to find this kind of devotion, wouldn't appreciate what you had to do to keep it, how much of yourself you had to surrender. And as her glossed lips work him over, the loathing rises up in him. Not just for himself and the woman who gave him so much and took even more, but also for the boy too. The pretty ones don't know, would never understand.

His breathing becomes erratic, and he moans, knowing his orgasm is coming, and he can't tear his eyes away from the body on the bed. For a brief moment, he wonders if the boy ever felt this, ever had someone he'd do foolish things for, ever had someone do things to him that made him forget all reason. He hopes so. Maybe then he'll be able to stop seeing the boy's eyes every time he closes his own. But then he's coming and he forgets all thought as she swiftly swallows the last bit of self-respect he has left.

He braces himself for the moment when she stands before him and looks into his eyes. He feels his eyes will reveal his revulsion, his fear, and his desire to flee and never return. Of course, he need not worry. She has no more time for him. She has a new pretty to add to her collection. She turns and stares at the boy before her.

"*Merci, mon amour*," she whispers.

He sees his chance for escape and slowly and quietly backs out of the tent. Her words following him out the door. *Thank you, my love…*

He hopes fervently as he makes his way to his tent that they are the last words he will ever hear from her. Even as his heart, and a much deeper place inside him, know they aren't.

About the Author

Tamela J. Ritter sits down everyday with one goal in mind: to write happy little stories about well-adjusted and loving families, about relationships that work, where no one hurts anyone else with their twisted desires and obsessions. She really does.

They just don't ever turn out that way.

Tamela's first novel *From These Ashes* was released by Vagabondage Press in 2013.

She can be found at www.tamelajritter.com.

A GRAVE TALE

Eddie Cantrell

1

Abel did not make a habit of disobeying his employer, but sometimes he just wanted to see a fresh corpse.

Mortimer Carroll, Sparrows Labyrinth's only mortician, had pulled him aside a week ago and said, "For the love of God, Buddha, Mary Jane Poppins, or whoever the bloody hell floats your boat, I want you to stay the hell out of here. You dig the graves. That's all. You have no business being in the embalming room or the mortuary. You make the mourners uncomfortable. You make me uncomfortable. I wouldn't be surprised if you even make the corpses uncomfortable. Just stay out!"

But for Abel, today wasn't just about the new corpse.

"Can't dig the stinking grave if I don't have the shovel," he mumbled to himself. "And I can't get the stinking shovel if I don't have the stinking keys to the shed, now can I?"

The keys had disappeared three days ago, and Mr. Carroll, or "Prickly Morty" as Abel called him behind his back, was taking his time with the duplicates.

So there Abel stood, slouched in the corner, dried snot smeared across his cheek, and his right eye, oddly bigger than the left, seemed to have a life of its own. With his filthy overalls, unwashed face, and ramshackle hair, Abel looked like he belonged in the clinically clean embalming room about as much as an amputated foot belonged on a dinner plate. Ignoring the occasional glare from Prickly Morty, Abel kept his attention on the woman. Viewings were not done in the embalming room for obvious reasons, but when the young woman arrived half an hour ago asking if she could have a moment with the body before the service tomorrow, Mr. Carroll made a rare exception.

Abel's employer made rare exceptions for pretty women. Maybe he preferred them vulnerable. And breathing.

Abel watched her from behind the filthy strands of his hair as she looked down at the corpse on the preparation table. His eyes scanned the swell of her small breasts and the delicate curve of her neck. Lingered over her quivering chin and the building wetness in her eyes. Saw the paleness under her blush and the dark sickle moons under her eyes.

Soft rasping broke the silence as Abel scratched his bushy beard. He shifted his gaze down to the smartly dressed, rosy-cheeked body lying on the table.

"Are you pleased with the preparation, Ms. O'Hara?" Mr. Carroll asked, poised a discreet distance behind her.

Ms. O'Hara blinked as if a bubble popped in front of her eyes.

"Yes. My father looks at peace. You've done a great job, Mr. Carroll."

"Is there anything else I can do for you?"

Ms. O'Hara took a deep breath.

"There is. It's the reason I wanted to see my father before the ceremony tomorrow. And thank you for making an exception for me. I know this against normal procedures."

She dug around inside her purse for a moment and brought out a small, black silk cloth. She held it like it was a bird with an injured wing.

"My father received it forty years ago," she said, unfolding the cloth. Using her index finger and thumb, she lifted up a small pocket watch and let it gently swing on the end of a delicate chain. A rich gold gleamed from its smooth and flawless surface.

Abel raised his shaggy head. The reflection of the gold pocket watch swung in that deformed eye.

Her lips started trembling again. "He became preoccupied with it. Obsessed. Never went a day without keeping it in his pocket. And the peculiar thing is it never ticked a single second." Her voice cracked as she said, "It was broken."

"When he was in the hospital, I took the watch to a specialist down in New Haven." Her pretty eyes welled up. "I thought if I gave it to him, and it worked, maybe, somehow, it would help him get better." She dropped her head, her face broke into strained creases and the tears fell, running down her cheeks in murky streaks. Mr. Carroll pulled a handkerchief, white as snow, from his blazer.

"Even in hospital, sick as he was, he mustered the strength to argue with me for taking it. Said it worked perfectly well. Said he could hear it ticking." Ms. O'Hara dabbed her eyes. "Anyway, the watch specialist in New Haven convinced me that it couldn't be fixed. Said it would never tick another second." Her eyes drifted over to her father's face and stared at it for a moment. "Too old, insides too damaged, too late.

"Would it be all right, Mr. Carroll, if I left it with him? I think they'd want to be together."

"But of course, Ms. O'Hara," Mr. Carroll said with a single nod. She tucked the gold pocket watch inside her father's blazer.

"I assure you, Ms. O'Hara, that your father is in good hands. This afternoon, Mr. Allen will prepare your requested lot at the top of the hill. It is truly beautiful up there. Most lovely view of the town." Mr. Carroll's eyes glared over the rims of his glasses. "Isn't that so, Mr. Allen?"

A crooked grin uncurled across Abel's face. "Of course, Mr. Carroll, sir," he said, staring at the spot on the blazer under which the pocket watch lay.

2

The burial grounds, with their lush, green grass, freckled with hundreds of crooked gravestones, stretched out behind the chapel and mortuary and rose up over the small hill. An apple tree stood at the very top of the hill, silhouetted against a sky ablaze with a melting sun. Limping and heaving, Abel made his way back down the narrow, cobbled pathway that meandered through the middle of the grounds. His lower back ached from having just dug the O'Hara grave, and the walk back down from the hill had been taken very slowly. He stopped for a breather halfway down and leaned on the shovel, singing his favorite folk song:

"Yeah, I'm goin' down, sir
Way, way down
Gonna sing this song
Deep, deep down in the ground"

He looked around at the tombstones on either side of the path, mumbling the lyrics over and over again. A fat crow landed on a gravestone within spitting distance and gave Abel an obnoxious caw.

"Don't like your tone, bird."

The crow cawed again.

"Caw, yourself," Abel shouted, and winced as a bolt of pain shot up from his leg into his hip. Damn leg was getting worse. Pain was spreading.

"What a pretty sight you've turned into, Abel, you crippled bastard," Abel grumbled. "Stinking gammy leg, screwball eye, back all twisted up. Becoming a stinking horror story cripple." He spat and winced again. "That stinking car crash left me a mangled-up bag of scarred skin and broken bones," he told the crow, who craned its head and let out an hysterical sounding barrage of caws. Abel swung his shovel at the bird and watched it launch into the sky in a scurry of feathers and more mocking caws.

He faced back the way he'd come. Abel easily spotted the apple tree and the fresh mound of dirt next to it. He shook his head, a seething grimace on his face. "Took me two hours to dig that stinking hole. Tomorrow, I got to shovel it all back again."

He wiped sweat from his forehead using his sleeve and continued walking down the hill. At the bottom, where the yard straightened out for a hundred meters, he stopped and looked up at the large white statue of Mother Mary, holding a blanket-covered baby in her arms.

Let the little children come to me and do not hinder them, for to such belongs the kingdom of heaven.

Abel looked up from the engraved scripture at the statue's base and glanced at the area behind it. The graves here were smaller than the others, decorated with flowers, candles. Some with cuddle toys. He skimmed the children's graves. One grave in particular caught his eye.

"Gonna sing this song, deep, deep down in the ground."

Abel approached the small wrought iron fence that separated the graveyard from the churchyard and mortuary. The gate squeaked as he slipped inside. He leaned the shovel against the fence, hobbled down three broad, concrete steps and stopped between the two buildings.

"Keep your watch, old man," he said, looking at the mortuary. Somewhere in there, Mr. O'Hara's body laid in the darkness of one of the five fridges.

"Don't have my keys anyway." Truth be told, Abel didn't feel like stealing from the dead man anymore. Not today. What he felt like doing was going home and opening the bottle of Old Smuggler whiskey waiting for him in his otherwise empty cupboard.

"Stinking watch is broken anyway," he said, giving the building a dismissive wave. Abel started walking to the exit at the end of the path. Then…

Tick-tick-tick.

He stopped.

"Huh?" he muttered, looking back at the mortuary. He heard it as clear as that mean old crow's caw.

"Losing my marbles."

He shook his head and limped off a little faster than usual.

3

The moon, like a giant, white mushroom head in the sky, dangled above the tiny wooden cabin. It stood, warped and wonky at the bottom of a dead-end road, plopped in the middle of a small yard overrun with weeds, glass bottles, scrap steel, and other useless junk. A warm yellow light flickered from a solitary dirty window. A loud guffaw broke the quiet of the street.

The inside of the house was spinning, so wonderfully, so smoothly, like a never-ending merry-go-round. Abel reached for the bottle, smiling a happy idiot's smile, watching his hand sway this way and that.

"Gotcha," he roared and broke into drunken laughter. "Now come to Papa." The bottle swayed precariously over the glass, spilling big splashes of whiskey onto the table. He filled his glass half-way up, lifted it to his lips, and vanished the whiskey in a single gulp. He shuddered as the alcohol burned its way down his throat. "There you go," he slurred.

He set his sights on the unmade bed at the other end of the room. The bed was only three meters away and a clear and straight path, but the stinking floor seesawed from one side to the other. Abel stood up on rubbery legs. His torso swayed backward and forward like a geriatric Elvis Presley impersonator.

"Of course I can walk in a straight line, Prickly Morty," he slurred. "I'll show you."

His hand glided up and pointed at the bed, setting his target. Then his upper body fell forward into a run, dragging his legs along behind him.

"Whooooaaaaaawwww," he howled as he zigzagged across the room, his clumsy feet thumping into the floorboards. For a short while, it looked as if he would actually make it, but at the last moment, he smashed into the foot of the bed, slamming face down on the floor. He lay dead still for a moment. A groan escaped his mouth, still squashed-up against the floor. He turned his face so he was looking under the bed.

He saw the white shoe box. That right eye bulged like a mad man's.

"Leave the box alone," Abel said. But his voice had changed, sobered in an instant. "Please, leave it alone. Please," his voice a pitiful whimper. Despite the plea, he watched helplessly as his hand glided toward the box. A big, salty tear built up in his left eye, rolled over the bridge of his nose and across the cornea of that mad, unblinking eye. The box slid toward Abel's face. He whimpered like a starved stray, and his face was a scarred and hopeless image of despair. He lifted the lid, reached inside, and held up a newspaper clipping. The manic eye darted over the bold headline.

Drunk driver kills eight-year-old girl

Abel rolled onto his back. He covered his face with trembling hands and cried. Not everyday blues crying, not the soft, dignified crying of mourners. Loud, guttural bawls heaved his gut and jolted his gaunt chest.

"You, you, you, you," Abel repeated.

And then he heard it again. Somewhere behind all the loud sobbing and incoherent mumbling, behind the nightmare flashes in his mind, behind the alcohol stupor, Abel heard it again. The soft, distinct, ticking of a pocket watch.

Tick, tick, tick.

4

A bel watched the procession from behind the apple tree. The socket around the right eye had turned an angry red and the eye itself, bigger and rounder than before, looked as if it was about to pop out of his face. In the distance, he heard the deep rumbling of thunder.

Someone tapped him on the shoulder, and he swung around with a gasp.

"Sorry, I, ah, forgot your name," Ms. O'Hara said. She offered a smile instead of her hand. He didn't know where to hide his dirty face.

"Um, Abel. Abel Allen." He put his hand out and immediately withdrew it realizing that not even Mother Theresa would shake it.

"I just wanted to thank you for preparing such a beautiful spot." she said, looking out over the town. "My father would've loved it."

Abel shrugged. "Well, I just dug the h—um, well, my pleasure, ma'am."

She nodded. "I wanted to say thank you, anyway."

Even though her eyes were tired, they were still radiant blue, and Abel willingly drowned in them.

"Lucy," a tall man from among the crowd called. "We need to go."

Ms. O'Hara opened her mouth as if she was about to say something more but then smiled instead.

"I'm sorry for your loss, Ms. O'Hara," Abel said. She turned around.

"Can you feel it, Abel?"

Abel frowned. "Can I feel what, ma'am?"

She stared at him, fixing him with sudden intensity.

"Evil, Abel. Evil."

Abel swallowed but kept his mouth shut.

"Be careful, Abel. Be very careful. I'm not sure why yet. But something is wrong."

She walked off, leaving him floating in the sweet scent of her perfume and the mysterious gravity of her words.

5

Abel stepped up to the hole and looked down at the partially covered coffin. Ignoring a dull throb behind his right eye, Abel began singing his grave digging song. This time the words held the heavy weight of a dark premonition.

"Yeah, I'm goin' down
Way, way down
Gonna sing my song
Deep, deep down, down in the ground"

The shovel dug into the mound of earth. Soon, Abel was pitching load after load into the grave. He could hear the hollow thud each heap of dirt made inside the dark depths of the grave. Even though Abel had become used to the sound, today it made him shudder.

His digging became more frantic. He sang louder. Dug harder. Ignored his aching bones.

The dark, heavy clouds that had been building on the horizon all morning began moving over the graveyard. Thunder rumbled through the sky like a monstrous thing up there was waking from a long slumber.

Abel had forgotten about the broken pocket watch now buried with its master. But beneath all the loud lyrics, he still heard it. Very quiet, very clear.

Tick, tick, tick

Each tick came out a little louder, more insistent. Some were short, quick sounds while others stretched out over a few seconds. Sometimes in the break between each sound, Abel heard something else. A whisper. A voice. Sometimes a male's voice, sometimes a female's, sometimes it sounded like something else entirely.

Tick…come…*tick*…get…*tick*…me…

Abel sang out even louder trying to drown out the sounds and the voices. His voice cracked and rose in pitch as each word left his mouth faster than the last, one stumbling out over the next.

"YeahI'mgoin'downwaywaydowntowherethemoonnevershines"

He shouted the lyrics at the top of his lungs, his shrill voice stirring the quiet of the cemetery. But the sound continued. When the grave was filled, he dropped to his knees, punched his ears with his grubby fists, and screamed the lyrics at the sky.

6

bel hobbled down Old Graves Road. Each step spat fire into his leg, a nauseating pressure was growing in his head, and he felt acid bubbling in his belly. Worst of all, the sound of the pocket watch showed no signs of abating. It only intensified, overriding his senses. A bird burst from a tree but instead of hearing its flapping wings, Abel heard only ticking. An ambulance raced past, and the siren gave off loud, drawn-out ticks. Terror and desperation contorted his face.

"Please, stop; please, stop," he whined, limping even faster.

Abel burst into his home and collapsed against the closed door. His heart rattled against his rib cage like a rabid rat in a steel box.

A disorienting cacophony of mechanical ticks assailed him like an invisible army of demons. His panicked eyes darted over the room.

He whipped his head around and saw shapes moving across the windows. A shadow bled through the crack under the door. His head swung around the other way, and he saw the white shoebox on the floor next to the bed. He jumped back. "What the stinking hell," he cried. The box was vibrating like a jackhammer. *Tickticktickticktick*

Outside, the heavens opened up, and the rain poured down. But it wasn't heavy drops that Abel heard slamming against the tin roof of his home, it was a million deafening ticks. He ran to the table, grabbed the bottle of whiskey, and downed what was left of the burning contents.

A pathetic, scared whine escaped his mouth as he stumbled over to the sink. He opened the tap to splash his face but snatched back his hands. The tap was gushing out hundreds of tiny cogs, wheels, numbers, and dials.

"Oh stinking shit, oh stinking shit, oh stinking shit."

Abel stumbled back, lost balance, and fell hard onto his buttocks, as a mechanical waterfall flooded over the sink and started spreading across the floor.

The entire world was ticking. Every tick created another and so they multiplied until trillions of ticks were bouncing around in his brain. Abel repeatedly smashed his fists into his ears, but every pound ticked. He shut his eyes, curled his knees up, and screamed. Yet all he heard tearing through the deepest chambers of his mind was *tick, tickticktickticktickticktickticktickticktickticktickticktickticktick.*

Lightning crashed outside, shaking the house. The whiskey bottle toppled off the table. It rolled along the floor and stopped in front of his face. Abel opened his eyes, still screaming and saw his horrified reflection in the bottle. His bulging right was no longer just an eye; it was a big, round pocket watch, pushing through the translucent surface of the eye. The eye socket oozed an oily black fluid.

He stumbled to his feet, ran to the door, and flung it open.

"Gonna, break you into a million pieces," he shouted, his eyes wide with panic and chest heaving. He charged into the raging storm outside, disappearing in the haze of Old Graves Road.

7

bel stepped into the dark churchyard. The ticking came to him in waves now, sometimes deafening while others fainter. His eyes adjusted to the darkness, but he needed to get his supplies from the shed. Luckily, he'd left it unlocked after the ceremony this afternoon. The rain howled, and he cringed as lightning walloped through the sky. For a flashing moment, the quaint chapel with its long crucifix steeple became a ghastly place where unseen things lurked behind the narrow, black windows, watching him from inside. He gulped and took a step back. Slowly turned toward the mortuary. In the gloom, it turned into a nightmare, a haunted building whose fridges stored the bodies of dead angels, their throats crudely slit, bloody crucifixes rammed into their eyes, entrails hanging from hacked-up guts, and wings mangled by an inexplicable evil that at this very moment sat waiting for Abel in the darkness of the embalming room.

Abel shook his head, turned around, and stared at the exit. The light from the street lamp glimmered in the rain that fell onto Old Graves Road. The road that meandered down through the forest, into Sparrow's Labyrinth, and out over the hills to places Abel had heard of but never been. He took three small steps toward the exit at the end of the short driveway and then stopped. With his head lowered and shoulders slumped, he turned away from the road and took a deep, unsteady breath. Slowly, he raised his head and faced the graveyard. Rain and tears streamed down his haggard face. He couldn't see it in the darkness but knew what he sought was there. He heard the wind blowing between the graves, picking up each one's story and whispering it into his ear. A blinding flash of lightning ripped through the sky like a skeleton's hand. Abel cowered back but saw the hundreds of tombstones, white and jagged against a black sky. He saw the grave at the top of the hill, and a cold chill passed through him as if someone had just walked over his own freshly dug grave. He took a deep but shaky breath and walked to the shed behind the chapel, making sure not to look at the long, black windows staring down at him.

8

He stepped up to the grave, shovel in one hand, ladder hanging over his shoulder, and a headband equipped with a light around his head. The beam of light moved across the epitaph on the temporary plaque.

In loving memory of our father and husband
RODRICK O'HARA 1941 – 2013
Dust thou art, and to dust thou shalt return,
but 'twas not spoken of the soul

Abel blinked and looked again.

In loving memory of our father and husband
RODRICK O'HARA 1941 – 2013
Tick, tick, tick, tick

The flashlight flickered for a moment and then died.

"Ah shit, no," he said in the darkness and gave the light a few hits using his palm. The light flickered, died, flickered, and then stayed on.

He read the plaque again and breathed a sigh of relief. And not just because the light came back.

Lightning tore through the sky just as the shovel rose up into the air and plunged into the soft soil. The ticking sped up. Abel's mouth opened, but no words came out. He tried again.

Abel started to sing, slow and shaky at first but then with more force, as it seemed to take his mind of the ticking. At least for the moment.

Abel descended further into the hole as shovelfuls of soil flew out in muddy arcs.

He battled the sloppy mud and the gushing water. In the pale beams of his flashlight, he saw streams of murky rainwater flowing down the banks of the grave. The water got into his shoes and sloshed around his toes. He smelled the strong musty odor of the wet soil, of grass and the zinc smell of the water. And he smelled rotting apples. The flashlight flickered again but stayed on this time.

"Damn you," he said through clenched teeth as his hands struggled to grip the shovel's slippery handle. His hunched body surged forward in the desperate need to destroy the watch, to stop the ticking.

"I'm gonna sing this song, till the end of time," he carried on singing. Abel arched back, wanting to get extra leverage as his arms raised up and then brought the shovel down. It slammed into the dirt and struck the wood of the casket. The singing stopped. So did the ticking. Abel stood very still for a moment, listening. He heard it again, but it was very faint now, somewhere in the background.

He scraped soil to the sides, and the beam of light swept across the dark brown surface of the coffin. Using the shovel, he knocked on the surface three times and waited. Abel wiped his nose and nodded to himself.

He stepped over to the foot of the grave, secured the ladder, and turned around, "Yeah, I'm goin' down, way, way down..." The flashlight flickered, "Goin' to where the moon never shines and angels don't fly," and then it died.

"Damn this stinking thing," he said and swiped it off his head. He rammed his palm into it three times. The light flickered once. He hit it again, hard, this time with his fist.

"C'mon, you damn, stinking piece of shit. C'mon. Please."

It didn't come back. He tried switching it on and off a few times. Nothing. Finally, Abel let the light fall, heard it hit the coffin with a sharp thud. He stood in the darkness. He couldn't see much other than the occasional flicker of reflected light from the rain. But he heard the sound of his panting breath, water trickling into the hole, and rain hitting the coffin. Those sounds seemed faint, close but in the distance. He started to step forward toward the head of the coffin and then heard something. He stopped. This sounded much closer. Not loud but close. He felt it under his shoes.

Three dull knocks. Like a fist knocking on the cushioned inside of a coffin.

"Oh my God."

9

He stared at the head of the grave, not moving a limb. His eyes slowly adjusted to the dark and made out the slick surface of the coffin. He waited, staring at the spot from where he thought he heard the knock. His lips and cheeks shivered uncontrollably from the cold, but his eyes remained more still than a dead man's. When no fourth knock came, Abel swallowed and took a slow, deliberate step forward. He stopped and looked back at the ladder. It stood there in the gloom like a stairway to heaven. Abel swallowed and turned back at the head of the grave.

"Gonna sing this song, down in the ground till the end of time," he whispered and slowly went about the task of clearing the sides and surface of the coffin. The ticking sound slowed and softened but was still there. With the job done, Abel dropped the shovel. Knees on the closed lower half of the coffin, Abel pulled the top lid open. It didn't open with a horror movie creak but, for one ghastly second, Abel pictured red glowing eyes staring back at him. That sight would've given his old heart a shock too much to cope with. The bad light made it difficult to make out any specific features, but Abel saw the vague form of the corpse's face in the darkness. It was like looking at a ghost's face. He heard rain drops hitting dead skin. Abel reached forward. His hand brushed over the blazer's lapels, feeling the hollowness of the corpse under the smooth fabric, and disappeared inside. It was like putting ones hand into a trapdoor spider's lair. He clasped the pocket watch. Touching it, feeling its coolness, sent shivers down his spine. He pulled it out and without even looking at it, raised it above his head. The tiny chain dangled limply above his head.

"Going to break you, good and solid." But his hand froze. He slowly brought the watch down and looked at it, squinting his eyes. The ticking stopped.

"Huh?"

His chest heaved, his drenched face contorted in confusion. Cocking his head, he listened. He could hear the rain and the heavy splotches hitting the corpse's suit. But no ticking.

"Can't be," Abel whispered. He brought the watch to his ear and listened again. Nothing. He shook it, brought it back up and listened some more. And again, nothing.

He stared at the watch a moment longer. He growled, raised the watch, and brought it down hard, repeatedly smashing it against the side of the coffin. It crunched under his hand. Little shards of glass shredded his palm, but he didn't stop until he no longer had the energy to go on. He slumped over, totally exhausted. He tossed the pieces onto the corpse's chest and closed his eyes. His shoulders relaxed, and he breathed in deeply, appreciating the quiet.

After opening his eyes, he turned around and stepped to the ladder without closing the casket. A tear rolled down his cheek. He wiped it away, looked at his hand and realized it wasn't a tear. A big, black blob lay on his palm. Abel froze. More gunk seeped out his right eye. He turned back to the corpse. A soft gasp escaped his mouth. "Oh Jesus, oh Jesus, no," he whimpered. Open eyes stared up out of the corpse's head. Its hand moved and grasped the broken pieces of the watch.

10

A bel felt the corpse's thrashing feet kicking against the inside of the coffin under him. He spun around and clambered out of the grave. In his panic, he leaned back to look behind him, and the ladder tipped. Abel screeched as he toppled off the ladder and landed flat on top of the corpse. Arms wrapped around his chest. Cold breath blew onto his cheek, and the putrid, rancid smell of apples filled the air.

"Gonna sing my song till the very end of time," a scratchy, terrible voice whispered into his ear.

Abel screamed and writhed. The arms came up to his throat, and fingers cracked as they tried to curl around it. Abel's hand searched for the crowbar, snatched it up, and swung it back over his head. Something gave a wet, sickening crunch, and the fingers around Abel's throat loosened. He jolted up and dashed to the end of the grave. Without looking back, he righted the ladder and scrambled up. "Helpmehelpmehelpme," he mumbled in pure terror as he reached the top of the grave. But hands clutched at his ankles. Abel kicked at them. The ladder rocked back, and he saw the edge of the hole, his only escape, falling away from him.

As the ladder fell, Abel leaped for the edge. A blood-curdling laugh below him split the air. In that hellish laughter, Abel heard his defeat. As his arms stretched forward, taut as steel rods, he feared the end had come. But his hands hit the surface, and his fingers dug deep into the soft, wet soil. He slithered out of the grave on his belly and immediately leapt into a limping run. Until a tight grip wrapped around his ankle. Abel fell, face slamming into the mud. He turned onto his back and saw it. Its hideous face was paler than a haunted moon. The crowbar jutted out of its forehead and evil raged in its eyes.

"Yes, sir, I'm goin' way, way, way down," it said again, and Abel heard nothing human in that voice. Clear, sludgy fluid poured from its eyes, ears, and mouth.

"Lemme go," Abel screeched, but he could do nothing to stop the corpse from pulling him back toward the grave. It dragged him further, and Abel's legs went back over edge. As he went down into the hole, a bolt of lightning tore through the sky and lit up the darkness of the grave. In that flash of white light, Abel saw a nightmare. Where the coffin had lain, there was now a swirling pit of black gunk that plunged deep into an abyss of darkness.

"Nooooooo," he cried, when in that thick, black whirlpool, he saw the bodies of thousands of screaming children, arms and legs flaying.

"No, please, no."

"Time to pay, Abel. Pay for what you did," the corpse said. A dark creature stared back at him, glowing yellow eyes, a razor-sharp grin that split open like an unstitched wound, and the thing vomited a gush of black putrescence. Abel saw a whole infant in the bile drop down into the black whirlpool. It made no sense but yet, there it was, real as it was illogical. The thing yanked Abel further into the pit. Legs kicked out and fingers raked into the ground, ripping off his nails. Abel tilted his face up to the angry sky, shut his eyes, and screamed a long desperate wail into the night.

"Oh, you are going to love where we are going now, Abel," the thing said, and Abel gave up the fight, stopped screaming, and let the dread fill him. He felt his body go over the edge, felt the rushing gunk on his legs, felt the tiny parts of all those children grabbing and pulling him.

Blinding white light filled the sky, but his eyes stayed closed. The thing dragged his body deeper into the whirlpool. The current whooshed against Abel, threatening to pull him under forever.

The light never vanished. Instead, it only got stronger. Abel opened his eyes and saw nothing but a blazing white light. His right eye was burning in its socket. He was waist deep in the whirlpool but lodged and sank no further. The thing, submerged beneath the black swirl, yanked, but Abel didn't budge. He looked up into the light despite the burning in his eye. A shape was standing at the edge of the grave, haloed in the blazes of that radiant white light. Something filled up inside Abel. Hope.

Another yank. This time up. The thing tried to yank him into the blackness but the overwhelming force from above kept Abel firm. Another heave upward and now Abel was up to his knees.

The thing exploded from the whirlpool with a hateful screech. He felt the awesome strength in whatever was pulling him out of the grave.

Another pull up and then another. The thing tried to yank Abel back but Abel kept rising. The invisible arms lifted him further and further out of the grave. He ended up in the intense light, only able making out a hazy kaleidoscopic image of the shape. The intense heat bellowed into him in hot pulses. He heard a screech behind him and rolled onto his back with a frightened gasp. The thing climbed out of the grave like a gigantic black crab. It opened its mouth, spewing bile and body parts. It grasped at Abel's ankle with a gnarled hand, its black talons bared. Abel shuffled back and into the shape behind him. It stood firm as a steel wall. The thing stalked Abel, ferocious eyes, fixed and venomous. The white light started to twist and swirl upward toward the sky, sucked in a cyclone. Abel felt the hot wind blast up and around him, felt himself being swept up. A pair of powerful hands pushed down on his shoulders, weighing him down. The graveyard darkened as all the light sucked up into this gigantic blazing twister. It stretched kilometers up into the air, drawing in clouds, rain, and even bolts of lightning. Abel stared, gob-smacked.

The radiant sphere of light twirled faster and faster. Abel was sure if the heavy arms weren't weighting him down, he would've gone flying straight into it. The creature roared at the light, its arch-enemy.

"MY GOD," Abel shouted, his voice barely audible over the thunderous noise. He turned his face into the shape, away from the violent wind. He heard it twisting faster and growing louder. The sound became unbearable, and he feared he was about to go mad.

"Make it stop," he screamed into the shape's legs. "Make it stop, please!"

The roar continued, reaching an intense sonic climax.

And then silence. A silence that hurt his ears and stilled his soul.

Abel looked out. Nothing. The sky was clear and calm. No sign of the storm or the strange cyclone. The creature was still there, in front of him, also looking up at the empty sky.

"What in the name of—" Abel said. He looked at the creature and the creature looked at him. It smiled—or at least attempted some terrible impression of one—crouched over, and leapt, talons stretched out before a mouth stuffed with curved, razor-sharp teeth.

That was when the world went white.

For a moment, Abel saw a blinding light and nothing else. In a split second, all that light seemed to implode into an intense, focused flash. It shot through the sky, came down like a bolt of lightening, and slammed into the creature as it crashed into Abel. It exploded in a splatter of black gunk. Abel stared out at the empty spot where the creature had been a second ago, his eyes round and unblinking. He looked down at himself with wide eyes and ran his hands over himself searching for any signs of damage.

Instead he got only the slightest hint of burning wood and something else he couldn't place.

The storm was gone. So was the creature. A silver wafer of a moon shone in a blue velvet sky and washed the graveyard in black crooked shadows. A calm stillness settled over the place. A gentle breeze blew through the graves.

He pressed his back up against the shape behind him.

Abel turned around. "I don't know what you just did but—" he stopped and stared up at the figure looking down at him. It was not some mighty glowing entity. It was not a majestically, all-powerful angel. It was a child.

And Abel knew she was only eight years old.

"Jamie," he said, his big eyes twinkled in the moonlight. "It, it..." The words couldn't form in his mouth at first. "It can't be."

The girl smiled. "It is," she said. "I'm here now, Dad. I've always been here. You just couldn't see me."

Tears welled up. His mouth trembled. He raised his hand and reached for her. Felt her little knees, her thin legs. His hand lowered down onto her small feet, and his fingers brushed over her toenails.

"But you're alive," Abel said, looking up at her, shaking his head. "My little girl is still alive."

Jamie's smile faltered. She bowed her head, and her golden locks fell down over her face. How many times since the accident had Abel longed to smell those locks again, to kiss her cheeks over and over until she shrilled with glee, to tell her a story one more time?

"I can't stay, Daddy. I have to go," she said. "They're waiting for me."

"Who's waiting?"

"The Glow Beings," she said and glanced behind her. Abel followed her gaze. Down at the bottom of the hill, inside the children's cemetery quarter, he saw four glowing figures floating above Jamie's grave.

"They said I needed to help you, Daddy," she said. "But we're leaving now."

"Where are you going?" A tear rolled down Abel's cheek.

"I don't know exactly, but it's where we all go after we die."

Abel looked up at her. He remembered how she had looked on the embalming table two years ago. Her peaceful face that ghastly pale color. That face had come back to haunt him every night since. But now her face looked so beautiful, so much like it was supposed to.

Abel lowered his head and tears poured out. He wrapped his arms around her legs, buried his face into her dress, and sobbed deep, painful sobs.

"My God, I am so sorry, my baby. It was my fault. All my fault. I'm a drunk," he cried. "You were in the car with me, and you were screaming for me to slow down, but I was drunk. I was always drunk. It was my fault, Jamie. Everything is my fault and…and I miss you. I miss you so much."

Jamie stroked his hair and then gently lifted his head up to face her. "Daddy?"

His chest heaved as the tears continued falling.

"I love you," Jamie said. "I always will."

This time, Abel slumped over. He didn't think he could cry anymore, but he did. After a long while, the sobs turned to whimpers, and his breathing calmed. He looked up and found himself alone. The graveyard was dark, but a strange electricity remained in the air.

"Goodbye," he said.

No answer came, but a slight breeze rose and rustled the leaves of the apple tree. Abel knew his little girl had left.

He opened his hands. A tear hung on the edge of his eye. A small pocket watch lay in his palms. Smaller and daintier than the old man's. He opened the clasp and read the inscription on the inside.

> *Happy 8th birthday, Jamie.*
> *May time lay blessed before you.*
> *I love you. I love you. I love you!*
> *Your Daddy*

He closed the clasp and stood up. The ladder and shovel lay across a neatly made grave. Abel frowned. He thought he'd have to fill it up again, but the job was already done. He looked back down at the pocket watch. It gleamed in the moonlight. His hand gripped it tightly as if he wanted to make sure it was real.

He turned around and started walking down the hill, realizing his leg no longer hurt. He stopped for a moment, spotting his reflection in a puddle of water. The right eye was no longer the size of a pool ball. He looked back at the watch.

"Happy birthday, Jamie," he said

About the Author

Eddie Cantrell loves writing as much he loves music. His favorite time of the day is when he sits down in front of the empty page during the early hours of the morning. (He is a total insomniac.) Alice in Chains or Pearl Jam blare in the background, and so the writing begins. He counts Edgar Allen Poe, Stephen King, as well as Steven Berkoff as some of his favorite writers. Eddie dedicates this story to his father, Theo, who would've given you his last dime, even if all you needed was a penny.

THE RED SHAWL

Steph Minns

That drive to the hospital, following the ambulance down the bumpy lanes, was one of the most terrible journeys of my life. Why did Jen have to follow me out there? Why had my stupid, interfering mother even suggested she come out to keep me company?

Something red, fluttering in the hedgerow caused me to shriek and nearly swerve into the opposite lane, but then I realized it was just a plastic bag caught up in brambles, not a shawl. Not the shawl I'd seen as I'd watched that dreadful figure on the cliff.

As I stepped through the door of the old wooden cabin, it felt like saying hello to a familiar friend, one who knew you so well you didn't have to explain yourself to them. The cabin had been in the family for as long as I could remember, perched on the cliff overlooking the vast sandy beach of Ainscliffe, Dorset. My memories of family holidays were full of happy scenes of playing on the beach, my brother helping me with over-ambitious sand castles, and of collecting shells in buckets to compare with the pictures in the *We Spy Beach Life* spotter's book. There had always been laughter, the greasy smell of sun cream, and gritty sand in the cheese and pickle sandwiches Mum handed around. Summers seemed to go on endlessly then, rolling out to the horizon like the ever-changing sea, and that beach had seemed to roll on forever too, back then in my mind as a child.

No one had been here in a long time though. As I creaked the door open, the last rays of winter sunlight on the table tops and chairs revealed a frosting of dust. My first job was a quick clean around, then starting up the little petrol generator in the back shed. When the tiny fridge juddered into life, I unpacked my supplies from the car. So here I was, alone, isolated by choice.

As I set off for a walk along the deserted beach, the wind began to pick up and the first snowflakes started to spiral down. The huge flakes hissed and faded away as they hit the salty sand, and I turned after a while to make my way back to the rickety wooden staircase that wound up the cliff face, my thoughts on hot chocolate. Glancing up at the scudding gray clouds, I spotted a woman in a red shawl up on the cliff above me, standing, watching the thrashing sea. Company I hadn't banked on.

Behind the cabin lay the woods, an old estate plantation that was still managed for timber. The only people here at this time of year, I'd assumed, would be the estate manager and his family up at the house. I'd seen no sign of activity in any of the other cabins dotted among the trees since I'd arrived. I lost sight of the figure on the cliff top as I concentrated on making my way back up the staircase.

Back at the cabin, I stoked up the wood burner and slipped an Ella Fitzgerald CD into my portable player. It was just getting dark when I heard a woman's piercing scream outside. It sounded just yards away, on the cliff. I froze, and it came again. Stepping onto the cabin porch, I scanned the line of scrubby gorse along the cliff top, concerned someone was in trouble. I couldn't see anyone but called out all the same.

"Hello! Hello. What's wrong? Do you need help?"

I was greeted by silence.

I walked the cliff for ten minutes or so in both directions anyway, peering over the edge. All I could see was the swirling snow and the rolling shapes of the waves pounding the beach below in the gloom. Snow had started to build up against the cabin porch as I stepped back inside to pick up my mobile to call emergency services. For the next twenty minutes, I watched the police searchlights scanning the woods and the beach, feeling a fraud when they reported back they'd found nothing.

"We've spoken to the estate manager, and he's certain no one is staying here except you," the local constable assured me. "As it's private land, it's unlikely anyone else would be here, unless they had access or knew the paths through the wood."

"Thanks for coming out," I muttered. "I'm sorry to have wasted your time."

Alone again, I tried to settle for the evening with a book. Eventually, curled in my duvet from home on a musty camp bed, I drifted into sleep.

I was bitter, and I recognized how corrosive that emotion can be. That's why I'd come here, to try to heal myself emotionally. Physically I was fine, if you consider a lead dancer with the National Ballet who can no longer dance as fine. The injury had healed well enough, but my career lay tattered on the floor like a ripped up tutu. I'd missed the world tour, my chance to shine across the globe, and acceptance of that did not come easy.

When my mobile rang on the Friday morning, I didn't answer it, knowing it would be Mum, again. "Why don't you come home for Christmas with us? How can you be all on your own in that old hut during the festive season?" We'd had all these conversations over and over until I was tired of them, sick of the well-meaning advice from my family, just craving peace to get my head together.

After breakfast, I wrapped up to go for a walk through the woods. That's when I heard the woman again, wailing as though racked with the most terrible distress, the shrieks drifting eerily through the trees. It was a bright winter's day, watery sunlight spearing down between the oak and birch to set the wet ground steaming. Soggy, skeletal leaves clung to my boots as I plodded among the trees.

"Hey, anyone here? Do you need help?"

It was a ridiculous question, I realized. Obviously, someone was here. I caught sight of a figure flitting ahead of me, darting though the sunbeams and trees, and I thought I saw a flash of red. Maybe it was the woman I'd seen on the cliff in the red shawl, someone who liked to walk here and deal with their troubles in their own way, in solitude, just as I was doing? I suddenly felt uncomfortable about trying to intrude into their misery, so I turned back, content to leave it alone.

Later that afternoon, I took a drive into town, back along the rutted track past the estate house, and a tall, blond, thirty-something woman flagged me down as I passed the gate. Pulling up, I wound down the window.

"Hi, you must be Sally," she said.

"Yeah. I'm guessing you're the estate manager's wife?"

"Yes, Alison. I hear you had an encounter with our legendary Banshee the other night."

"Banshee?" I asked.

"Yes. The screaming." She seemed a little uneasy as she said this.

"Ah, that. I was worried someone had fallen down the cliff face and was in trouble, but the police didn't find anyone," I explained.

"No, they said as much," Alison replied quietly.

I sensed she was uncomfortable about broaching the subject, and I became curious.

"So what is the Banshee?"

"Local people believe the woods are haunted by an evil spirit. It's said to have been responsible for a number of deaths over the years, a child found in the woods that had run away from its mother, then a couple of walkers only last year discovered on the cliff path. Every time there are unexplainable deaths, people say they hear the screaming and wailing. I've never heard it myself, although my husband thinks he has. He's really into local folklore though."

She laughed nervously, as though suddenly embarrassed at what she'd just said.

"Well, my family never mentioned any rumor of it, I don't think, when we came here on holidays. Maybe they just didn't want to scare us kids," I shrugged.

I started to wind up the window, hoping she'd take the hint as I was keen to get to town and investigate the cafes and bookshops.

"If you need anything, just knock," she offered, smiling and gesturing back toward the house.

"I will, and thanks."

I revved the old Renault forward over the muddy ruts to continue my trip to town.

Driving back after a pleasant afternoon browsing the shops, a poetry reading session caught my ear as I flipped channels on my car radio. A languid voice murmured, as though intending the lines only for the ears of some intimate confidante.

From dark nights and broken dreams, new ideas can grow,
Unfurling as fresh leaves in spring, new paths to be trod,
Inspiring new-born forms to flow.

I found the words deeply moving, having been through dark nights and broken dreams myself lately, and my anger and despair had clouded and blackened my thinking. Usually a positive person, I resolved myself to sit down when I got back to the cabin to think my situation through rationally with notebook and pen. After all, I had other skills besides dancing, hadn't I? I was only twenty-five, and there was plenty of time to build a new career.

I sat enthusiastically scribbling notes until the sun started to sink into the ocean, turning the sea beyond my window to shades of gold, cerise, and finally deep violet. A sea mist started to roll in as I put together some supper from my deli purchases of the afternoon, olive bread, cheeses, and local cured ham.

Then the horrible scream came, loud and piercing, as though just outside on the cabin porch. Unnerved, I peered through the window, my first thought being that it was the distressed woman from the woods again. Then I thought of the tale Alison had told me that afternoon but scolded myself for my silliness. Bogeymen and ghost stories were just the stuff of local tourism. But when the second scream came, it dawned on me there really was something eerie and unnatural in the noise, as though wrung from the vocal chords of something inhuman, something from some other dimension.

Peeping round the curtain, I saw a figure standing about twenty meters away on the cliff, staring directly at the cabin window. The gathering dusk and sea mist partly shrouded it, but I was able to make out a white face, long straggling dark hair, and what looked like a red shawl clutched around the shoulders by white, skeletal hands. It was wearing, bizarrely, what I thought was an old print dress in a sixties style and flat red pumps. The eyes appeared as dark pits, and the mouth hung open in a silent O, as though about to emit another bloodcurdling shriek. Something about it, the way it stood, the lolling head on a neck too long for a normal person, gave me the chills. But I was fascinated, mesmerized by it, and somehow I found myself walking toward the door, about to open it and go outside. As I reached for the latch, I suddenly checked myself in horror. What was I thinking? Instead, I bolted the door and retreated to the window to sneak another look out, wondering if it could see me silhouetted by the lamp light.

The figure stared silently at the window for a minute or two, as though weighing something up, before taking a few steps backward to hurl itself over the edge of the cliff. It didn't drop with gravity like anything of any weight, but seemed to flutter for a moment like a handkerchief caught up by a breeze, the red shawl flapping around its shoulders, before it vanished from view, dropping just like the gulls that swooped over the cliff edge to wheel above the waves. I let out a small shriek of my own.

Shaken, I sat up most of the night, terrified it would return. What would have happened if I'd opened the door, had not shaken off the glamour it had cast over me for that brief moment? A terrible feeling of dread consumed me, and as soon as the sun rose I started packing up the car to leave, cutting my break short. My rational mind was desperate to try and make some sense of what I'd seen the previous evening, but whatever it had been, I just couldn't spend another night alone here.

I'd just switched off the generator when I heard the whine and pop of a scooter pulling up outside. Walking back round the side of the cabin, I found my younger cousin, Jen, standing on the porch, grinning like a demented Cheshire cat, her hair spilling wildly from under a woolly hat. At twenty-two years of age, she still insisted on wearing cartoon T-shirts better suited to children. Today it was Deputy Dawg's visage, distorted almost beyond recognition over her massive DD chest, peering from under her padded jacket. Jen and I didn't have much in common, and she'd grated on me with her selfish, attention-seeking dramas over the years. Jen had been responsible for much of the family troubles in the past, stirring and tittle-tattling, running back and forth between family members, and I didn't really encourage her friendship.

"Jen," I tried to sound bright. "What brings you out here?"

"Aunty Sal said y' might need some company, so I hopped on me scooter."

Her shrill, put-on "cool kid in the hood" accent jarred on me like sand paper.

"I was just about to leave actually."

Her face dropped like a kid whose lolly had just been taken away.

"But I've come all this way to see y'," she huffed.

"Come on in then," I offered. "I'll put some coffee on."

I tried not to show my irritation as her eyes scanned the hut like a nosy shrew. Another hour before setting off wouldn't hurt, I guessed.

"Aunty Sal said you were staying out here over Christmas," Jen rattled on. "So why are y' packing up to go home? Bit too cold for y'?"

I gritted my teeth at her braying laugh and felt foolish, unable to give the real reason, that I'd been scared like a kid by a supposed phantom.

"No, just stuff to do at home," I forced myself to reply politely. "Sugar?"

"Yeah, two please. Any biscuits?"

Deputy Dawg's inane toothy grin challenged me across the cabin as we made small talk, mostly me listening to Jen's endless moans about her boyfriend, her friend who wasn't her best friend any more, and the new manager at work. As usual, it was all about her. I don't think she even asked me how my ankle was doing. When she finally finished her coffee, I rose and suggested we lock up as I was keen to head back to the city before the snow got heavier. Large flakes had begun to drift down again outside, and that was the best excuse I was able to come up with.

"Okay, I can take a hint," Jen sniffed. "But I want to just take a quick walk to the point first. I've not been out here for years, and I wanna see the old haunts where we all used to play. You comin'?"

"No thanks, I'll just finish packing up the car," I replied. "Be careful on the path. The snow's getting heavier."

"I will." She shrugged on her puffer jacket. "Won't be long."

I watched my cousin heading off along the cliff path toward the point where the lighthouse stood, hunched into her coat, bobble hat pulled down over her ears. I waited an hour, but Jen did not return from a walk that should have taken her no longer than twenty minutes at most. Concerned that she may have fallen and was lying hurt in the snow, I pulled on my own coat and set off to look for her. I walked to the point and past that, calling Jen's name, as the snow swirled thicker and the icy North Sea pounded the beach. The cliff path was deserted, and I peered hopefully every now and then over the cliff edge to check she wasn't down on the beach instead. No one was on the beach, not even an intrepid dog walker. As I turned back past the lighthouse, its red and white finger stark against the snowy sky, that blood chilling, inhuman scream slit the air.

I froze and peered nervously behind me, back to where I thought the sound had come from. It had not been Jen's voice. A figure was walking purposefully toward me along the path. The falling snow partly concealed it but even from a distance, I was able to make out the red shawl and the unnaturally long neck, the dark pits of eyes and straggling dark hair. I lost the last shreds of my nerve and fled. Glancing back just once, I realized it had stopped following me, but I still kept running, my ankle thankfully holding up. Once locked safely inside the cabin, I called emergency services to report my missing cousin.

"She should have been back ages ago, and I'm scared she's fallen and is hurt," I stammered, not voicing my real fear, that Jen was alone out there on an empty cliff with something fearful, something unnatural. I felt ashamed now for abandoning my cousin and fleeing, wrapped up in my own instinct of self-preservation.

Courage bolstered by the noisy arrival of a police car and rescue team twenty minutes later, I ventured out to explain what had happened and watched them set off along the cliff and beach. The team leader asked what Jen had been wearing, and I struggled to remember. All my panicked mind could conjure up was that stupid Deputy Dawg T-shirt. I was sure that something dreadful had happened to her, something connected to that awful figure, and I cursed myself for letting her go off alone.

∵   ∵   ∵

The police found Jen's body half a mile down the coast, broken on the rocks below the cliff. I wasn't allowed to see poor Jen at the hospital. A policeman explained that she'd tumbled over sharp rocks and it was best I didn't. He said there would have to be an autopsy as there was possibly foul play involved.

"Foul play? You mean someone pushed her over the cliff?" I nearly said "something," but who would believe me if I voiced my growing suspicion?

"Did you see anyone on the cliff top or in the area today?" the policeman asked. "Anyone wearing something red?"

"Red?" My stomach knotted into a tight ball.

"We found your cousin clutching a torn piece of red wool, maybe from a scarf or something similar. It could be from her attacker's clothing if she tussled with someone."

Or perhaps from a red shawl, I thought, with growing horror.

ABOUT THE AUTHOR

Steph has been a keen reader, writer, and artist since childhood. Originally from the suburbs of London but now living in Bristol, U.K., she works part time as an administrator and spends her spare time writing. Steph's previous incarnations have included council parks gardener, magazine editor, and web designer. Her dark fiction stories range from tales set in dystopian realities to ghost and horror. Her publishing history includes several short stories and a novella, accepted by notable indie publishers Dark Alley Press, Grinning Skull Press, and Almond Press. Competition wins include the Dark Tales March 2014 international competition and an honorable mention in a Darker Times horror/dark fiction 2013 competition. Steph has a website—stephminns.weebly.com—where you can read free stories, interviews, and reviews. She's also a member of the Stokes Croft Writers group, which runs free story-telling nights in Bristol bars, called Talking Tales.

Phoenix

J. S. Watts

A soft pop, like the sound of a gas jet discreetly igniting. An explosion of eye-branding brightness and, for a blessedly short moment only, a pain-flayed scream.

The wind was bone-achingly raw. It rushed over the field with enthusiastic vindictiveness, sucking the heat from everything it touched. Detective Constable Alison Lumen shivered, though she wasn't sure whether it was from the icy chill of the wind or because of the grotesque tableau spread across the blackened grass in front of her. Despite the wind, the smell was enough to make you shiver or retch, or both: a heavy aroma of smoke, soot, and burnt meat.

There was a body, little more than ash really, but somehow holding to human form. Flakes of black and gray flesh were being caught by the wind and blown in circular eddies around the remains and the rest of the crime scene. At least, everyone was treating it as a crime scene. It was still not clear what it was, but human bodies tended not to combust spontaneously in the middle of an open field in the darkest part of the night.

The wind gusted again, and Alison pulled her too-thin coat round her naturally slim frame, but then had to let it go again in order to clear her mousey-blonde hair away from her face—a pattern of motions she had been repeating for at least the last twenty minutes. Bloody wind.

"Bracing, eh?" one of the firemen, still hanging round the scene, called across to her.

"Bloody cold, more like" replied Alison. "What do you think burned him—slash—her to a crisp like that?"

The fireman walked over to her. He was a nice enough looking bloke, though he looked almost too young to be a fireman. "Like my gaffer's already told your gaffer," he nodded his head in the general direction of the tall, overweight presence of Alison's Detective Inspector, "we haven't a Scooby. We're waiting on forensics as much as you. Whatever it was, though, was both fierce and focused. Your Jane or John Doe was incinerated in the open air, but it's only the grass immediately surrounding the body that's scorched. They were felled where they stood or were already dead when they were set alight."

"Could it have been natural, like a lightning strike?"

"All things are possible, I guess." The fireman shrugged his broad shoulders. "But I've never seen lightning burn like that and, as far as I know, last night was cold and storm-free; no thunder and lightning to do the business."

The conversation stalled, and Alison retreated back inside her inadequate coat. Under his fire-fighting gear, the fireman looked fit, in more ways than one. He didn't seem to be suffering the way she was, but then, Alison had always felt the cold. She could have gone back to her car to wait—she'd a nice warm car blanket there—but knew she'd get yelled at by D.I. Finnegan. It would be the perfect excuse, and he didn't normally need excuses.

"At least the location's appropriate."

"Eh?" Alison emerged from her self-pitying reverie to peer at the fireman still standing beside her.

"I said, at least the location's appropriate."

"In what way is this frozen, wind-swept field west of nowhere an appropriate place to barbecue someone?"

The man pointed to the middle of the field. "See that footpath running across? It's the old parish boundary and just beyond, almost exactly where your John or Jane Doe has been crisped, is the site of the town gibbet. Mostly it was hangings, but it was also where they executed Alice Lunt."

"Sorry?" The conversation was ceasing to make sense to Alison.

"From your accent, I thought you were local. You must have heard of Alice Lunt, the last witch in the county to be burned alive at the stake?" Alison shook her head dubiously and the fireman continued, "A solitary woman, apparently, living on the edge of things, she was accused of killing one Jeremiah Warner through the use of witchcraft, specifically by using magic to hurl a lightning bolt at him. Needless to say, she was found guilty and her punishment was devised to fit the crime. She was burned alive right here in this field. Quite a local legend."

Alison stared at the blackened remains in front of her and shivered for the umpteenth time. "I don't know about appropriate, but I still say it's bloody cold and bloody grisly. I've never seen anything like it."

Another time, another location: an exposed hilltop, or what passed for a hill in the flat, weather-scoured terrain of the county. Despite the wind, the cloying smell of smoke and charred meat was strong.

Alison pulled the wind-blown wisps of hair away from her face and looked down at the two bodies, little more than ash really, but somehow holding to their human forms. Blackened bone was visible where the flesh and skin had split. This time, she felt seriously, about-to-throw-up, nauseous. Two burnings in as many days and three blackened corpses. They had only just managed to identify the first one as Rob Saggers, a local poacher, and now they had two more badly burnt and unrecognizable bodies on their hands.

Alison hunched down within her insufficient coat. The wind was as bitter as ever, and forensics were taking their own sweet time. D.I. Finnegan was deep in conversation with the pathologist and had made it clear he wouldn't be needing her any time soon. She couldn't begin to remember why she'd been so keen to come out to this incident.

Over on the other side of the hill, the fireman she had chatted to last time was standing on his own. She walked over toward him.

"We meet again," he said.

"Looks like. Anything you can tell me about this one?"

"Very similar to last time, except now there's two bodies. Fierce, intense heat, tightly focused on our char-grilled human barbecue."

Alison's nausea worsened. "Do you have to?"

"You used the barbecue word last time."

"Yes, well, I didn't this time, and now I also can't say I haven't seen anything like it before. The repetition makes it worse."

The fire officer grinned. "Not the only thing to be repeated."

Alison raised her eyebrows in query.

"They've picked another good spot for it. This place is known as Beacon Hill, an ancient bonfire site, part of an old fire-signal chain running north and south down the eastern side of the country. North of the town, here, you get a clear line of sight for a long, long, way."

The fire officer seemed almost smug of his knowledge. Alison was not sure why, but it put her off asking him his name or if he wanted a drink at the end of his shift.

It was a whole week before the next fatal bonfire. During that week, there had been a significant lack of progress on the first two cases. They still didn't know who the second set of corpses were or how the fires had been caused, let alone by whom, and there was talk of bringing in a specialist team from London to take over the investigation. As the station wags would have it, D.I. Finnegan was "fuming" at needing a team from "The Smoke" to "smoke out" a local fire-starter. Alison found both Finnegan's anger and the crass humor unsettling and was grateful when it stopped, but as it only stopped when four more people were found crisped in a burnt-out car, she felt guilt at her sense of relief.

"It's not your usual car fire," said Alison's friendly fireman, who, she was pleased to note, was once again at the scene. "It has the hallmark of the other two incidents. Fascinating stuff."

"Do you make a point of turning up to all these fires?" asked Alison somewhat archly.

"It's what I do. Do you make a point of always turning up and then standing back on the edge of things?"

Alison winced internally. "It's what I do."

They were standing beside the main bypass, where it skirted the east side of town and ran for a little way beside a large bowl-shaped indentation in the landscape. The wind blew down the road with a scything cold that felt as if it had crawled there all the way from Siberia. Alison had piled on extra jumpers this time, but still felt cold to the bone. The winter had been a long one and showed no sign of warming up, even though it was now officially spring.

Alison hugged herself more closely, stamped her feet to get some life back into them, and said, "As my Dad used to say, I guess when your number's up, it's up. There's nothing you can do about it, but I'd hate to go like this. What a way to die. It doesn't bear thinking about, but I guess I've got to. So what else can you tell me about this incident?"

"Everything I told you about the others, except this time they were in a car and the exploding petrol tank makes working out what took place even more difficult. There doesn't seem to be any significance to the location, but otherwise it fits Verner's theory—" He stopped abruptly.

"What? What's Verner's theory? Why haven't I heard about this before?" Alison glanced over at Finnegan, in the center of things as usual, and wondered if everyone else, except her, had already heard about it.

"Oh, it's nothing really," The fireman appeared to look slightly embarrassed. "An old guy I'm friendly with. Used to be a fire fighter, but's now retired. His name's Verner."

"And he has a theory?" Alison's sarcasm was audible.

"Well, yes. You know the thing: you can take the fire fighter out of the fire, but you can't take the fire out of the fire fighter. He's a bit odd, I guess, but still interested in things, fire-related things, I mean."

"So what's his theory and why haven't you mentioned it before?"

"Wasn't sure at first what we were dealing with. Wasn't sure you'd take it seriously."

"And why might I not?"

Alison found out exactly why she might not take things seriously when she mentioned Verner to D.I. Finnegan at the next team briefing.

"Verner? That old crack-pot? You're having a laugh, right? Who put you up to this?"

Alison colored softly. "No guv, I just thought...I mean...one of the fire officers mentioned him and..."

"Well, if I were you, D.C. Lumen, I'd give up on thinking. It doesn't suit you, and I'd leave that fireman well alone. You really couldn't cope with a whole one." The briefing room sniggered. "Know his name yet or did you spread 'em without asking?"

Alison crimsoned with embarrassed heat. She'd taken her fair share of locker-room humor in the past, but from the boss and in front of everyone else was different. Finnegan, seemingly intent on pulling her to pieces publicly, took a deep breath prior to a further tirade, when a group of four dark-suited strangers walked into the briefing room. He fell silent, and his face blackened noticeably. Alison guessed they were the specialists from London.

One of the four stepped forward and held out her hand. "D.I. Finnegan? I'm D.C.I. Brand. I gather you need some expert help?"

There was not a flicker of change on Finnegan's already scowling face, but Alison could feel the tension in the room increase. Surprisingly, he responded civilly, at least for him. "Been told you lot know your arson from your elbow, and we could do with a bit of that round here."

D.C.I. Brand laughed. "Indeed we do. So what progress have you made so far?"

Alison, knowing the total lack of progress made, expected Finnegan would struggle answering the question, but, without missing a beat, he swung back round and pointed decisively at her. "D.C. Lumen here has developed a lead from amongst the local fire-team. Seems one of their retired officers has seen this sort of thing before. She's just off to interview him."

"Good stuff," said Brand. "Do a thorough job and report back to me when you've done." Finnegan grinned, and Alison found herself dismissed and on her way to interview Frederick Verner.

Verner was not what she was expecting. White haired, yes, thin, but well muscled and clearly fit, only lightly wrinkled and with clear, piercingly bright blue eyes. Not her idea of an OAP at all. He didn't seem elderly or eccentric, but Alison felt there was a sense of dark gravitas about him, an air of having seen it all and possibly too often.

Alison began by questioning him about the fires, but somehow it ended up with him asking more questions than she did. It was not long before he knew the minute details of each of the three crime scenes, her pained frustration with D.I. Finnegan, her discomfort with the prolonged wintry weather, and more about her disappointing personal life than she usually shared with anyone. All she knew about him were his outline theories on the fires, and, though she didn't want to admit it, they were starting to sound a little bit far fetched. Things had started off sensibly enough, though.

"Well over fifty years ago, it was. Another fearsomely cold winter, just like this one. It felt as if all the heat had already been sucked from the earth, but the winter just carried on carrying on. I was new to the job, bit like your Josh is now." Alison made a mental note that her fire fighter friend was called Josh. That was one bit of information at least, and hopefully something she could put to positive use later. "We was feeling the cold big-time, but then we got distracted by the fires. First one was at the old Clunch Pit, just one dead and burnt, but then the other fires quickly followed: north, west, south, and east again. The Beacon, Gibbet Field and Chapel's Farm and, with each fire, the body count doubled. The last fire left sixteen dead in one night. We were waiting for the sixth fire, but as suddenly as it started, it stopped."

"Why was that, do you think?" interrupted Alison.

"I has my ideas, but nothing was proved." Verner did not sound as if he entirely believed this.

"So what were your ideas? Why the pattern? What do you think caused the fires? The fire teams say the heat is exceptional, but can't say what causes it."

"That'd be the way of it. Didn't know then; can't say now. What I think is just opinion, like."

"So what *do* you think?" Alison was getting frustrated and trying not to show it. She was failing.

"They laughed then. You'll laugh now. Best I keep it to myself."

"No. Go on. That's why I'm here: to hear your theories."

"Well, if you're sure?"

Alison nodded encouragingly and waited. Frederick Verner resumed his narrative. "The fires are connected. Then and now and to one another. And linked to earlier fires: Beacon Hill, an old bonfire site; Gibbet Field, the site of the witch burning and the place where the witch was said to have earlier incinerated her victim—before then, it was the place of the Samhain fires; The Clunch Pit was the site of the old Beltane bonfire, and Chapel's Farm has been subject to more arson attacks than make sense. Always losing hay ricks and the like, as well as barns and out-buildings. That's a lot of burning for one small town. Most places would have had the Beltane, Samhain, and beacon fires in the same place, but not here. No, we have fires on all major points of the compass, just like you've got now."

"Yes, but there's a difference between planned bonfires and what we've got now. Plus we've only had three," Alison pointed out.

"Won't be long before Chapel's has another fire, then."

"How can you be so sure?"

"It's the pattern of them: north, south, east, and west and so on, all on the old fire sites and, if you looks back, there's been these sudden fierce fires every fifty to seventy five years, and each time there's been a multiplying body count. I was struck by the pattern when I saw it then and researched back. This town has had a lot of fires over the years. It's been passed off as Corn Law protests, Napoleonic spies, witchcraft and acts of God. Go back far enough, it was the rampaging of old Queen Boudicca, but it's always fire and there are always multiple dead. Back in the middle ages, the church burnt down and took forty-eight souls with it. Now that would have been a fire to have seen."

Alison ignored the enthusiasm in his voice. "Well, that undermines your theory. The church is nowhere near your four fire sites."

Verner seemed disappointed, like a favorite pupil had got her sums wrong. "Not now it ain't, but back then it was. Why do you think Chapel's Farm got its name?"

"Because the farmer was called Chapel?" Even as she said it, Alison knew it was the wrong answer. She moved on. "So what do you think is causing the pattern? Copy cat arsonists? How many people are going to remember what happened fifty or more years ago, let alone earlier?"

"Oh, I doubt people will, but the land does."

"The land?"

"Yep. She's got a long memory, that one."

"So, what are you trying to tell me? The fires are geological or that inbred memory is causing them?"

Verner frowned and looked, yet again, as if she should have known better. "Inherited memory is human. Your arsonist ain't."

It was at this point that Alison realized she'd been had, that Verner was almost certainly barking and that she'd have to return, tail between her legs, to D.I. Finnegan and, now, to the fiercely-efficient D.C.I. Brand. Verner, however, just kept on talking, his theories about what seemed to be fire spirits growing wilder and wilder to the extent that she stopped listening. Eventually, she managed to make her excuses and left.

She took a long time getting back to the station. It took several cups of strong coffee in a nearby coffee shop before she could work out a way of reporting back that sounded almost reasonable. In fact, she tried hard not to report back officially, but D.C.I. Brand was adamant she needed a formal report. So Alison concocted a fictional story of a frail elderly fireman and developing Alzheimer's that meant whatever information Verner had once had was now lost. That sounded more plausible than the apparent spirits of Verner's theories (assuming that was what he had been going on about) and, she felt, almost justified her initial enthusiasm for exploring them. At least she now understood why no one else was seriously linking the current incidents to anything in the past. D.I. Finnegan just smirked when he read her feedback, but for once said nothing.

Alison tried to forget her experience at Verner's until a minibus carrying eight people burst into flames south of the town, on a lane that skirted Chapel's Farm. It was carrying eight fire fighters. Josh was one of them. The other seven were also local men and women.

The crime scene was gut-wrenchingly funereal: no black humor or even day-to-day chatter, just dark, intense focus by police and fire crews, but the increased intensity didn't yield any further information. It was yet another fire caused by unknown and inexplicable heat. Someone mentioned the word "unnatural," and a sergeant from the London squad was heard to mutter terms like "military" and "laser." "Unnatural" had a different resonance for Alison. She found herself thinking about Josh and repeatedly recalling Verner's strange ramblings, what little she could remember of them.

These flashbacks continued to distract her. On her way home that night, without even thinking about it, she found herself outside Verner's door. She was surprised to find herself there, but Verner didn't seem surprised to see her.

"Come in. Didn't think you'd be able to stay away for long. It's the pull of the fire's truth: as strong as gravity."

It was too cold to hang around outside. Alison walked straight in and didn't waste time on social niceties, "There's been another fire. Eight people this time. I… knew them. All fire fighters, including Josh. It's become personal. The specialists are flummoxed and starting to use the word 'unnatural.' So is it unnatural? You seemed to be saying it was."

Verner shrugged his still-broad shoulders in a surprisingly casual manner, "No, just the opposite. It's not unnatural. Hyper-natural or supernatural, maybe, pre-dating what we now consider to be natural, but not unnatural, oh no."

"So what is it? Explain to me again: what and why and how to stop it."

"That's a tall order from someone who didn't listen last time, and, anyway, it's complicated. What happens next depends on how you react to what I tell you. You didn't believe me last time. Why are you going to believe this time round?"

"Because I've nothing else to go on, and your ability to predict events seem uncannily accurate, so you must know something."

"And now you want me to predict what'll happen next?"

"Something like that."

"And if you don't like what I predict?"

"I'll worry about it if I believe it."

"Fine. It's your game now. It's very simple. The fire will keep spreading and the death toll will keep doubling until we do something about it." Verner looked at her knowingly.

"We? Us? Why us? What do you know that you haven't already said?"

Verner's face contorted and darkened. "I thought I'd ducked my responsibilities fifty years back, but what goes round, comes round. You've reminded me of that. There's no escape."

"What do you mean?" Yet again, things weren't making sense to Alison.

"It's best I show you." He stood up with surprising sprightliness and hurried upstairs. When he came back down, he was clutching an old corroded toffee tin to his chest.

Alison didn't know what she was expecting him to produce from the tin, but it wasn't the rough, black pebble he put into her hand. It looked like blackened pumice, but felt smoother, heavier and colder—icy cold. Whatever it was, an attempt had been made to carve it. It was so roughly hewn that at first Alison couldn't make it out, but as she followed its contours with her fingers, she decided it was meant to be a flame. As soon as she realized this, the shape of the stone became clearer, and she was staring at a living, black flame, flickering in her hand. She blinked in shock, and the flame was once more just a small lump of oddly carved black stone.

Alison glanced up at Verner to assess his reaction and found him staring at her, his pale blue eyes shining fixedly. "You saw it, didn't you?" he said. "You saw the fire inside the stone."

"What was it?"

"The truth. Flame attracts moths. The fire in the stone calls them. You and me, we're this season's moths. We are drawn to the burning, and either we control it or are burned."

This wasn't making any more sense to Alison than Verner's ramblings at her last visit, but she had seen something in the stone that made her listen.

Verner plowed on with his explanation. "The earth chooses. It calls to people born on this land and gives them the power and the duty to serve the fire within it. Fifty years ago, it should have been me, but it was Bill Blake who answered the call in my place. It was he who made things right then."

"But why?"

"Why did he make things right?"

"Yes, no, why create 'moths' to control a fire? Why the fire in the first place?"

"That's like asking why the wind or why the sea. There is water. There is land. There is air. There is fire. Each has its servants. Why are some people so attuned to water they can sense it in the soil and rock? Water divining is an age-old tradition of the land. So is this. So are we. It's what is. I was called like you are now, but I didn't take the shout and more died until someone else took my place. He made the burning stop then rather than me. We've got to do it now, or the burning will continue."

"But what is it we have to do?" Alison was confused, tense, and more than a little wary, but when she looked at the lump of black stone in her hand, the lunacy she was listening to somehow became sense and the only possible response to an increasingly impossible situation.

Verner responded to the confusion he must have seen on her face. "Look inside yourself and tell me. The answer's there. If you've been called, you'll know deep down, below the level of reason. If you don't feel anything, then I've got it wrong. I'm on my own, and there's no point talking no more. The shout's mine anyway, but there's always been a second person left on the land to channel the power until the next time. I thought it was Josh, but it weren't. You're the one what saw the flame in the stone." He paused and peered intrusively into her face. "Go home. Think about what you've seen, and if you know the answer, can feel it like a hot coal burning inside you, come back tomorrow and we'll talk more." He plucked the black stone from her hand and almost lovingly returned it to the tin.

Alison gasped. With the removal of the stone, a weight she hadn't known had been there was lifted from her hand. Suddenly she was light and unburdened but, at the same time, cut adrift from the world, like a balloon being lifted up and away from the ground on a gust of wind. It was as if she didn't belong anymore, and she left Verner's house reluctantly and uncertainly.

Back home, her usual routines felt like walking through a dream: everything, except the constantly nagging cold, felt distant, unreal and insubstantial. She went straight to bed but was shivering uncontrollably and couldn't sleep. All she could think about was the flame she had seen dancing on her open hand. She needed to see it again. When she finally drifted off, her night was haunted by fiercely burning flames, alternating with a heavy blackness so thick and airless, not even the light of the fire could penetrate. She woke next morning still cold, bone-achingly tired, and already late for work, but with an understanding of what she should do seeping along her veins like scorching acid. For once there was no hesitation.

She was back at Verner's house before she'd had breakfast, but there was no answer to her knocking, and the door was firmly locked. There was no point in going to work. She would have already pissed off D.I. Finnegan by being late, and she now knew her real vocation was here, stashed and waiting in an old, battered toffee tin. The need to hold the stone again was growing. It was hers now, not Verner's. She got back in her car and waited, wrapping herself in the car blanket in an attempt to stay warm. It worked, but the warmth made her sleepy, and she was soon fast asleep.

She woke with a start. The sun was already dying down, and she was numb with cold. How long had she been asleep? Confused, she got out of the car and returned to Verner's front door. There was still no answer to her knocking, but now the door was unlocked. She walked in, drawn instinctively upstairs to where she had last seen the toffee tin and its lump of black stone. The tin was there, open, and the stone was squatting on a folded sheet of white paper. He had left it out for her. It was hers. Grabbing the stone and clutching it tightly in her left hand, she read the note Verner had left:

"You're here. I knew you'd come. You're drawn to the fire like we all are. It's an addiction; there's nothing the same as it and there are such benefits: we burn brighter and longer because of it. You'll see, but letting go is difficult. I couldn't manage it last time, and people died in my place.

When the fire comes, it burns until satiated. One of us as a glowing sacrifice, or numberless ordinary victims: one way or another, it gets what it wants. Eventually one of us burns, and the other remains behind to guard the dormant flame until the next hiatus. There's power and a very long life in it for the one who remains, but also a scourging knowledge of their ultimate fate. It's a difficult knowledge to carry inside you.

Last time I couldn't bring myself...left it too long and someone else took my place. This time has already gone on too long. I know what's got to be done. I've gone to the Gibbet Field. You'll find the truth there, along with your destiny."

The black stone seemed to be pulsing in her hand. Alison didn't stop to think: by now she was beyond thinking. In a daze but with a growing sense of urgency, she got back in her car and drove in a hurry out of town to the place of the witch burning.

It was deep dusk and growing darker by the minute. Amid the thick gray and confusingly interchangeable shadows, Alison picked her way over the rough field. She could see a white glimmer spread across the footpath. She made her way to it and realized it was a white cotton bedsheet laid out across the ground. Close up, it wasn't perfectly white, but was smudged with gray markings and a dark, poorly drawn circle. There were four dark mounds of something holding down each corner of the sheet and an even darker shape in the center of the circle. She touched the mounds. They seemed to be piles of ash, and the dark shape in the center was a larger version of the carved stone she still held in her hand. She gripped the smaller stone all the tighter. It felt warm and comforting against the clinging cold of the darkening night.

There was no sign of Verner, though in the thickening, primeval darkness it was difficult to see anything much beyond the edges of the sheet. Alison wished she had brought a torch with her, but it had been morning when she had started out and there had been no need. She clutched the small stone in her left hand tighter still.

She wondered if Verner had already offered himself to the fire in order to send it back into the earth for another half-century, but there was no sign of a body. She was considering with growing concern the source of the ash when she heard muffled footsteps coming toward her. She sensed it was Verner before he spoke.

"I'm pleased you came. Last night, I wondered if I might have to bring you."

Something in his tone made her feel uneasy. She gripped the pebble in her hand all the more firmly. This made her think of the larger rock at her feet. She swiftly scooped it up, feeling its weight in her grip. As soon as it was in her hand, she noticed the noise. First an extended, gentle hiss like a slowly released sigh. Then a soft pop, like the sound of a gas jet igniting, and afterwards increasing steadily in volume like a protracted and controlled exhalation, which became a meeting and merging of air, a rapidly rustling breeze, and then a rising wind.

Verner was close to her now, in the gloom just beyond the edges of the sheet. The wind was close to roaring. He was yelling to be heard above it. "She's coming. I knew you wouldn't be able to resist touching the rock. You called, and she's coming to you. For *you*. You're this lifetime's servant and sacrifice."

Alison peered at Verner through the heavy murk, trying to make out the expression on his face. "What do you mean? What's happening?"

"You've touched the mother stone and initiated the summoning. She's coming for you now, not me."

"But I don't understand."

"There's nothing to understand. All you've got to do is die." And with that, Verner stepped rapidly into the ash ring, violently shoving Alison out of it. His movement was unexpected, and she stumbled onto the grass of the field. It was then she saw it: a fiery streak of light, like a vertical slit in the black of the night, seemingly an inch or two long, but burning longer and brighter by the second. No, not longer, closer. It was growing because it was rushing closer, a glorious streak of light, at times almost holding to human shape, but elongated and with a ripple of light around the head and shoulders like a pair of wings, or like a magnificent incandescent bird in full flight, or maybe just a huge pale candle, blazing the whole length of its wick. It was fiercely beautiful, but already it was almost too bright to look at.

From within the ash-drawn ring, Verner was screaming at the oncoming blaze, "Embrace her. Embrace your obligation. Her power shines through you, illuminating me as I watch and wait." Belatedly the truth hit Alison with the impact of a lightning bolt. Verner intended her to take his place, to die, so he could gain another fifty or more years of extended life, life that should rightly have been hers. He'd done this before, at least once.

The light was blinding. Alison squinted through watering eyes at the advancing brilliance. What should she do? She understood now why Alice Lunt might once have wielded lightning. Maybe there was a way to channel the blinding power and overcome Verner, but Alison didn't know how. She hadn't had the time or opportunity to study things. What she had thought she knew had been felt within her gut and now, gripped by shock, she couldn't feel anything. Only one thing was clear to her: Verner could have stopped things sooner and limited the death count. Verner should be facing down the fire now in her place. She should be where he was, watching and waiting. If she was going to die prematurely and in his place, she was damn sure he wasn't going to get away with it again.

She swung round, turning her back on the advancing burning apparition, seized hold of Verner, hitting him with the larger rock still in her hand and fell backward out of the circle, dragging Verner with her. They both stumbled into the oncoming inferno. There was sudden all-consuming heat. Skin darkened, blistered and split. Agony gripped Alison in a cauterizing hold. She could hear Verner shrieking in agony and her own, higher pitched, faltering wail. Then an eye-branding explosion of white–hot brightness and, for an all too brief moment of pain-free transcendence, everything finally made sense before the hot, unending darkness swallowed her.

About the Author

J.S. Watts lives and writes in Cambridge in the U.K. Her poetry, reviews and short stories appear in a diversity of publications in Britain, Canada, Australia, and the States and have been broadcast on BBC and Independent Radio. To date, she has had four books published: a debut poetry collection, *Cats and Other Myths,* and a subsequent multi-award nominated poetry pamphlet, *Songs of Steelyard Sue,* both published by Lapwing Publications and two novels, *A Darker Moon*—a dark, literary fantasy, and *Witchlight*—a paranormal tale, both published in the U.K. and U.S. by Vagabondage Press. For further details, see www.jswatts.co.uk.

ART OF THE LIVING

Michelle K. Bujnowski

"...it is possible to construct an apparatus which will be so delicate that if there are personalities in another existence or sphere who wish to get in touch with us...the apparatus will at least give them a better opportunity to express themselves...."
—Thomas Edison, Scientific American, 1920

Notebook in hand, Isabelle Riviera sauntered into the conference room. A secretary followed with a tray of coffee and scones. The meeting had been arranged for nine o'clock on a Friday morning at an estate lawyer's office called Vincent & Associates, located in Manhattan. A man rose to greet Isabelle and her husband, Michael.

"Good morning," Maurice Vincent said. He had been the person to contact them on behalf of his client.

"It's not good yet," Isabelle mumbled and reached for coffee as Michael winced, apologetic. She immediately opened her notebook and wrote down the date and time.

"Please call me Maurice," Mr. Vincent continued.

"My name is Michael Riviera, and this is my wife, Isabelle."

"Your reputations precede you. I'm impressed with your backgrounds," Maurice said, smiling.

"Thank you," Michael said. "We were surprised at your invitation. We're used to larger audiences."

"So it would seem," Maurice said. "I've looked at a few of your published papers. Very interesting. When I showed one of your web lectures to my client, Harry LaFleur, he wanted me to call right away."

Maurice noted the two appeared handsome together, and each had the look that they'd rather be at the library.

"Why did you need to find us?" Isabelle said, cutting to the chase. Isabelle had short, straight, dark hair, with pale skin that glowed. Her eyes were piercing, almost black. The sternness of her nature contrasted with the ease of her husband. He appeared to have a Latino ancestry with short, black, wavy hair that worked well with his thin frame.

Maurice cleared his throat, uncomfortable. "Let's just say there is mounting evidence that something needs to be done with one of my client's estates. I deal with many of his family properties; however, this one in particular poses a problem for my client."

"How is there a problem?" Isabelle said.

"The house…something there hurts people."

Isabelle and Michael smirked. Maurice was grave.

"You think I'm joking."

"No," Michael said. "We think it rare, or likely improbable, to find a ghost capable of inflicting physical pain."

"I want you to prove me wrong. If the house proves you wrong, however, can you help remove it?" Maurice wiped his forehead with a handkerchief.

"Would you rather a Catholic priest?" Isabelle said.

Michael gave her a stern look.

"Thought I'd ask."

A young man with messy red hair strode into the room. He took off his coat jacket and set his suitcase on the table before shaking hands.

"I'm Harry LaFleur. You must be Isabelle and Michael Riviera, the great paranormal scientists. Nice to meet you both."

"If you don't mind me asking, why do you need our help?" Michael said.

"I don't mind at all. It's a fascinating place with incredible history. The oldest generations of my family lived there: my grandfather, great grandfather, and so on.

"Unlike my forebears, I don't wish to reside in New Jersey. I'm too busy here in the city. Therefore, I need someone to take care of it.

My Aunt Mildred watched over the house until last week, until our gardener went through an upstairs window and died. No one in the local area wants to work there now."

"Suicide," Michael said.

"It isn't likely," Maurice said. "There is a landing with a railing fifteen feet from a large window that spans the second and third floors. He would have had to launch himself to break the central part of the window and land twenty feet into the backyard. The glass is too thick. Police are baffled."

"And so are we," Harry said. "That's where you come in. Your studies are impressive. I'm sure you could figure out if there is a supernatural...uh...presence, from what Maurice has shown me."

"The likelihood of finding such a poltergeist may be nonexistent," Michael said.

Isabelle continued to take notes, a line of concentration on her forehead.

"You mean a class five poltergeist? Harry said. "I'm quoting your own work. Have you never seen one?"

Isabelle sighed and set down her notebook. Michael cast another warning look. She gave a sigh of consternation and leveled with them.

"We have seen class one through four," Isabelle said. "Class one is akin to a feeling or sense that one is not alone. Class two involves actual sight of an unknown presence. Class three is where an unknown presence causes movement of an object. Class four: the presence can talk to humans, usually with a wide range of emotion left from previous life.

"Class five was created due to the evidence we gleaned from sources all over the globe indicating presences that can cause destruction on a massive scale. None has been documented with instruments, only with witness accounts. We did indicate that class five was a theory, not something that we'd observed. You're putting words in our mouths."

Harry smiled broadly. "Tell me, would the fifth be able to throw a human through a window?"

"If a spirit did that," Michael said, "it would be a great deal more powerful than anything we've seen."

"Well, this is what you've been waiting for," Harry said. "You can prove your theory by staying at my house. Otherwise, we may find the killer responsible."

"I'm inclined to agree with the latter," Isabelle said. "It likely involves a human. The house is in Jersey. Anyone in your ancestry of Italian descent?"

Harry chuckled. "If that's the case, the mob might be easier to get rid of."

Michael felt Harry's demeanor too nonchalant for the discussion. "Joking aside," he said. "We're not entertainment. This is science for us."

"How is that?" Harry leaned forward. "I've done my research. EMF and EVP are standard, mist photos are extras. All of which have results that are highly controversial. Why has anyone believed in your work?"

Isabelle shut her notebook and rose to leave. Michael knew the drill. His wife's mood swings were part of the deal. She couldn't be so open to let in the deceased and filter out the living. She went into the hallway.

"We have what others don't. My wife's sixth sense."

Michael leaned on the wall next to Isabelle. Her eyes were closed. He looked at her with sympathetic sensitivity that could only have grown from a decade of marriage and work together.

"We got the job," he said, smiling. "We leave for Connecticut this afternoon." He pushed her hair behind an ear. Her eyes opened.

"Goody." She glowered behind a mask he knew well. The story of the LaFleur ghost had touched a nerve. He wasn't sure why. There were things from her childhood he knew she hadn't told him. It was the wisdom with which she spoke at times that made him think her insights weren't just from sensing the dead; they came from firsthand experience.

"He's not what's bothering you," Michael said. His eyes probed hers. Her mask darkened. She looked past him down the hall. A flicker of hate darted across her features, but when she looked at him again, she looked frightened.

"We don't have to do this, honey." He put an arm around her.

"I don't think it's real, but if it is, it could be the most challenging job we've had. Or if there is a killer out there with a vendetta, we could be in danger."

"They just said they have astounding security in the house. That's what alerted the police, of course, but *after* the gardener went through the window."

"Hmm, comforting." Isabelle said.

The couple went to their home in Queens to pack as agreed. Used to prepping for short trips, the equipment was always ready to go inside the garage door.

The drive with Harry LaFleur was entertaining as well as frustrating. The fact that Harry was driving them in a convertible with the top down on a beautiful summer day did not make up for the fact that he yelled the entire drive. He rambled about nothing. Isabelle felt he was hiding something.

Isabelle understood pretense: everyone had it, no one knew this better than she. She smiled in moments it was expected, laughed when necessary, spoke as little as possible to get through conversation so it would ultimately end. She enjoyed few people; Michael was one of those rare persons with whom she relaxed.

Harry, on the other hand, used words to obscure himself and confuse those listening. She felt the real Harry might be thoughtful. As they drove closer to the house, she began to realize he was more nervous, jittery.

She enjoyed scenery from the backseat, glad to be further from the tirades, however, Harry tried to make up for the distance by twisting and shouting over his shoulder. They left the city with light traffic and, in two hours, made it into green rolling hills, trees interspersing the landscape. Isabelle felt the sun on her skin, closed her eyes, and listened to the wind. It ruffled her hair and began to feel less like wind. She shivered as the sensation flowed over the rest of her body, cold and liquid. Gasping, she felt engulfed by water. It was cold as ice. Opening her eyes, she saw she was surrounded by darkness. She felt water ripple past her skin as if she were in a current. Michael and Harry were gone, and she heard nothing.

Isabelle screamed but felt water move into her windpipe like an icy claw. Reaching for where Michael must sit in the car, she saw her father appear before her. He was holding a carving knife from their kitchen, blood dripping from the blade. A maniacal smile curved his lips.

"What do you think about the presidential candidates this year, Isabelle?"

She opened her eyes and saw the sun and both of the men looking at her with concern as she breathed heavy, shaking. A horrible headache filled the space between her eyes.

Expecting to spit out water, she managed a response instead. "They're all bullshit."

Harry guffawed and pounded the steering wheel. "Exactly!"

She rubbed her temples. Michael recognized the occurrence of a vision and handed over a small packet of two pain pills. She took them dry and swallowed, hating her gift. What had happened? She had been drowning as surely as the sun shone. Then a memory of her father resurfaced. Isabelle hadn't thought of what he had done in years.

The car tires crunched gravel. Isabelle snapped her head up. Harry stared at her in the rearview. Red fingerprint marks glowed at each temple.

"We're here," he said, hesitant.

Good, Isabelle thought. *I've already frightened him. Maybe now he'll stop babbling.* She stumbled out of the backseat after Michael moved the front seat forward.

They gawked at the stone mansion. She could see a river winding behind it; further back was a forest Isabelle would die to explore. Her heart made an enthusiastic leap, a rarity. Enormous hedges surrounded the age-darkened stone. Flowers bloomed from every corner of the lawn. Michael grinned.

"Are we in a Hitchcock film?"

She winked and pulled out her field book.

"What year was it built?" She dug out a pen.

"1812. Five years after my great great grandfather, Arnaud LaFleur, got into the coal industry in Pennsylvania," Harry said. "You can imagine the grandeur of his lifestyle."

"I can imagine more than that," Isabelle said under her breath.

"Yeah, we should up our fee," Michael whispered. She smiled, and he looked happy to see it. Her cheeks hurt from lack of use. The men grabbed the bags and equipment and went up the walkway. Isabelle scanned the windows. She reached outward with her senses and found quiet.

Harry unlocked the front doors and chuckled when they groaned inward, the cliché obvious. The hall into the foyer gleamed of cherry wood. Picture frames held grainy and dust-covered family photos. Dust motes danced in the sunlight. The hall opened into a marble atrium with a grand staircase spiraling out of view. Other passages led off the big room to the rest of the house. Isabelle continued to take notes.

Michael set down the equipment. "Is the power on?"

"Yes," Harry said. Michael opened one of the small black Pelican briefcases and pulled out an electromagnetic field detector. He turned it on and left them abruptly to scan the house.

"What's that about?" Harry asked.

"Trifield EMF," Isabelle said. "It senses changes in electromagnetic fields within a range of approximately twenty-five feet. Supernatural sources have a general range of disruption that we use as a reference; anything higher or lower is considered man-made or environmental. It can also sense a moving electromagnetic field." She smiled at Harry's discomfort. He cleared his throat.

"Very interesting. Does it work?"

"If you hear the alarm, it's likely an electric source," she said. "That's why he's checking the house now, so we aren't given a false alarm later by a power outlet or other obvious source."

"Has it worked with spirits?" he said.

"Do you always harass the help?" Isabelle wrote down descriptions about the general presence of the house. "Yes, it has helped to locate them; however I usually don't need it, but it can corroborate my visions."

"You see them?"

"Yes, usually. Harry, are you going to tell me why you're nervous?"

"I don't know what you're talking about."

"Oh, I think you do," Isabelle said.

He sighed. "This house has a bad history. I'm afraid of what you'll find."

"You believe it is haunted?"

"I've heard stories from my aunt, but no one has ever believed her. Not even me, until lately. The gardener last week…what happened wasn't possible. I saw the body." He grimaced.

"Are you afraid to be here?"

"Yeah, I guess so."

"You should leave. Go stay at a hotel, for your own good." She turned away.

"I'm staying here with you," he said, following Isabelle. "You need my help. Jesus, you must be better with the dead than the living."

"I'm not very good with either," she said. "Why do I need you?"

"I've heard stories from Aunt Mildred."

"Right, it would be good to learn them. Okay, but be careful; don't get too emotional. Michael and I need to remain objective."

Isabelle carried the rest of the equipment to an office where she set up two computers on a large mahogany desk. She heard a series of beeps to signal her husband's location upstairs.

Michael poked his head into the office where Isabelle was turning on software. Harry sat in an extra chair he pulled in.

"Let's go out back and check out the window the gardener went through. This place is huge; it'll be a workout to scan every few hours," Michael grumbled.

They followed him into the dark hall, through a nearby door, and downstairs into a day-lit basement. Already, Isabelle could see the lush landscape of the backyard through windows along the back of the house.

Outside, their feet met a yard that began a gentle descent into granite bedrock. The rock served as shoreline at the edge of a wide murky estuary that drained into a sound, eventually the Atlantic. A line of mud marked where water had reached high tide hours ago. There were no trees in the backyard but plenty in the pine forest beyond the river and clusters straddled both sides of the house.

"*C'est bon*," Isabelle said. "We could make this a vacation."

Harry smiled. "If we make it through the night."

She raised an eyebrow. Turning where she stood, Isabelle looked back to the house. A gaping maw stared back. The center of the house held a twenty-foot wide window, three-stories tall.

"Nothing popped up when I scanned the central part of the window, but of course the landing in front of it doesn't get very close, maybe fifteen feet away," Michael said.

"That's the window he went through?" Isabelle said, unbelieving.

"Yes, you see how improbable it is that the gardener, John, did it on his own. He went through the second floor level," Harry said. "Twenty-five feet from the ground in the center of the window. The glass was an inch thick. It was shipped from England in 1812. We replaced it last week with modern double-paned glass."

"I can't imagine the cost," Isabelle said. "Who could throw themselves through that?"

"I have nightmares of the body," Harry said. "Police showed him to me to confirm his identity."

"Nightmares. Anybody unusual in the dreams?" Isabelle said, matter of fact.

"No."

"Sorry, Harry, that's horrible," Michael said. "This happened at night?"

"Why was he inside?" Isabelle said.

Harry swallowed. "That is the question, isn't it? He tended the grounds, never needed to go inside aside from accessing his equipment in the basement. He did die at night, around two a.m. I heard a rumor from my Aunt Mildred that he had been acting strangely. He would talk to himself and stare up at the house."

"This aunt kept an eye on the place?" Michael asked.

"Yep, the infamous aunt who told me stories of this place when I was a kid."

"Let's scan the landing site of the gardener, and then Harry can fill us in with the history," Isabelle said.

Michael proceeded to walk the backyard where the gardener had landed. Isabelle watched Harry's face as Michael strode by, holding the meter. Harry was pale.

"Are you going to be all right?" Isabelle said. "You don't have to be here."

"I guess I'll have to be okay. I was six when Aunt Mildred started telling me ghost stories about this property. Those stories gave me night terrors for years. I had to endure counseling and medication in my teenage years. In college, I began to forget my fear, let it go as an old woman's means of excitement. I healed and moved on.

"I became successful. Last week, John's death brought it all back. Can you imagine a thirty-five year-old man with night terrors? But at least I can face the problem with sanity. My aunt lost any sense she had and went from living on her own to a nursing home a few days ago. I had to put her there. I have to put a stop to it, face my fear. Maurice didn't find you; I did."

Isabelle smiled. "Maurice is a good friend, isn't he?"

"I'm glad you're here, Isabelle, but I hate having you around. Worse than a shrink."

"At least you had someone you could talk to, even if you did pay them," she said, watching Michael.

Harry looked at her. "What about your husband? You share your burden, don't you?"

She looked up at the house, smaller windows like tiny eyes around a giant mouth. "Can't share everything." The image of her father with the knife resurfaced. The memory confused Isabelle. Why did it keep coming back now? Michael walked back to them.

"Not a damn thing," Michael said.

"Let's walk to the river and hear Mildred's tales," Isabelle said.

They sat on a stone bench. A salty tang hung in the air. Before them, the river had been reduced to a mud flat. A puddle sat in a crook, and, the flat swept eastward out to sea beyond their line of sight.

"I'd like to know if Mildred's stories are true," Harry said. "That's why you're here. My Aunt Mildred grew up here as a child. I always believed she told them because she loved tall tales, but my mother said she became obsessed as a child and has been odd ever since.

"Their parents had to pry my aunt from the room in the attic where she played by herself. She failed in school but kept busy with her own projects. She later became a recluse when she moved from the house. Never married."

"Need to check the attic," Michael said. "Totally forgot."

"What was she like when she told stories?" Isabelle said.

"My mother would pick Aunt Mildred up to get her to socialize, much to my detriment. Mildred would wait until Mom was out of the room to really shine. When she told them, she would stare into space.

"She would clutch my shirt and whisper these monstrosities, vehement. Some stories were nonsense, babbling. Some were clear. Those eyes…deranged; gray hair stuck out in every direction.

"She said she had seen a woman raped during a party at the house, watched another man get pushed down the stairs during a separate party, and swore she watched a child drown in the pool inside. Here's the thing: no one ever died in the house while she lived there.

"I've done research in the past few years. A woman never reported being raped, but one went missing in 1816. A little girl did drown in 1835. A man died falling down the stairs in 1838. All three happened during ballroom parties a hundred years before Mildred was born. My mother thinks she became delusional, but these deaths did happen here."

"She played in the attic?" Isabelle asked.

"Yes, my grandmother said she would go from the attic to get food from the kitchen, go to the bathroom once in awhile, but mostly stayed there all day."

"Did she say who did these things?" Michael said.

"That's what terrified me as a boy," Harry said. "She kept saying it was someone she couldn't see. Even as an older woman, she believes this. The only exception was the raped woman. Aunt Mildred said she saw a man on top of a woman in a nice dress but couldn't see their faces."

"Did she give any names?"

Harry shook his head. "I didn't ask, didn't want to know."

"Can you show us where these things happened according to her?" Isabelle said.

"Just the pool where the girl drowned. Like I said, I didn't ask specifics as a six-year-old."

"Was anyone ever implicated for these crimes?" Isabelle said.

"A governess was charged for negligence when the girl drowned on her watch. However, it was considered accidental. Nothing ever came of the missing woman. The man who fell down the stairs was considered a drunk, another accident. It was hard to decipher old records."

Michael nodded, obviously concerned. The fear was palpable in Harry's voice.

"You said she babbled. What would she say?" Isabelle said.

"Jeez, she rambled on about rippling walls, so many strange things like that."

"Anything else?" Isabelle was writing.

"She talked about faces in the glass, that exact phrase, can't forget it. She warned of portraits in our home that held stories I shouldn't watch. Last thing I remember—she said to make sure the faces of people didn't change. What does that mean?"

Isabelle looked up with a sharp inhale. "It could mean…a variety of things."

"Such as?"

"I truly don't want to influence you," Isabelle said. "In general, the spirit may have been communicating with your aunt, trying to get her to see what it wants. She would sound delusional to a rational person."

"Well, then I hope Aunt Mildred is schizophrenic," Harry said. "Otherwise there is something in there hell bent on talking. That's all I know. That, and I won't be sleeping tonight." He got up and started for the house. Michael rose with him. Isabelle felt light-headed and closed her field book.

"We won't either," Michael said. "But we're not paid to sleep. We should set up our equipment for nighttime. We have a few hours before dark." He grasped Isabelle and pulled her into his arms.

"Everything all right?" He said into her ear. "Something is agitating you more than normal. We don't have to finish the job. We can walk away."

"I don't know what's wrong. I want to help Harry. I know what it's like to be haunted your whole life."

He sighed. "Why won't you talk to *me* about it?" He shook her shoulders gently.

"Only one of us needs to feel haunted, Michael."

Michael went from room to room, placing EMF sensors that transmitted wirelessly to their computers. It was four o'clock. Isabelle walked the house, describing framed photos and paintings to her recorder. She was taking Mildred's advice seriously. Harry may have called it babbling, but she felt they might be true observations.

She noted all the mirrors in the house. She never believed in the superstition that they could show the dead but wouldn't discount Aunt Mildred on that count either. Isabelle never knew how spirits would make themselves known. Most of the time, they showed their memories to her and remained invisible. Sometimes they portrayed their death with little interaction, which was enough for her.

Their repertoire had been established by people who touted that she could exorcise spirits; however, she felt they owed their success to record keeping. No one else could document the dead, not really. Isabelle had investigated many "seers" and found their documentation unfounded. They had yet to meet someone else like her.

Exorcism was the wrong word. Isabelle merely acknowledged the presence of a spirit. Few words were said on her part. Each spirit held a certain resistance to change. In their reports, she assigned class levels indicating that resistance. Most fell into classes one through three. They had never dealt with a presence that may have caused a death, if at all possible.

By seven o'clock, she had a hand cramp from writing and found Michael as he finished setting up sensors. They heard noise coming from the kitchen where Harry was making a salad. He nodded toward boxes of pizza next to a bottle of wine.

"Wow, Harry," Michael said. "You did all this?"

"I can't take credit," Harry said. "My staff brought the food, but they refuse to stay. It's just us three now."

The kitchen had a large island with bar stools. A brick oven filled a corner of the space, a chimney extending up through the house.

"This is the brightest room in the house, since it was updated ten years ago," Harry said. "The rest of it is plain ugly. I hate old wallpaper. Isabelle, did you see the mosaic in the dining room there?"

"No, I didn't make it to the dining room. This place is huge," she said, between mouthfuls of pepperoni slices. "It's not like me to forget something like that. I need to walk the attic as well."

Michael nodded in agreement. Harry handed them plastic cups of wine.

"I shouldn't have alcohol," she said.

"Why not? Interferes with seeing the dead?" Harry said, mouth stuffed.

"Quite the opposite," she said.

"Isn't that a good thing?" Harry said.

She rolled her eyes. "It's hard enough to tell reality from their world half the time."

Harry stopped chewing. "Can you tell me about their world?"

Michael shook his head. "I get a rare glimpse as it is; she won't tell you."

"Sorry for asking, but why don't you talk about it, Isabelle?"

"I tell or write as much as needed for academic purposes," she said. "Anything beyond that could be taken out of context. Some things would be enlightening, others detrimental, depending on how it's received."

"You bear the weight for all of us then?"

She rose, took her field book, and walked into the dining room. She had had enough. Harry stood to go to her.

"Don't," Michael said. "She does carry a lot. I see expressions, usually of anguish, and I'm sad to say I'm relieved I don't see what she does. I couldn't withstand being witness to traumatic events over and over. Her strength is one of the things I love about her."

"We see horrifying events all the time on the news, in movies; it's the bane of human existence."

"Not the same. She feels everything these spirits felt. News reels don't show you what it's like in a third world country. They get your attention for twenty seconds, and it's over before you can process it."

"True enough." They each tipped back a glass.

Isabelle walked the short distance into the dining room and turned to the right. A mosaic covered the wall, literally the entire wall behind a twenty-foot long table. She gaped at a mass of fragments arranged as a river beneath a star-laden sky at twilight. An oak frame held the mass. The fragments ranged from angular to rounded, millimeters to several inches, each held different designs or colors, but the overall effect was mesmerizing in its unity.

The river was a collection of blues and off-white tones. Green and gray pieces lined the shore as rocks and grass. A blood orange mass showed a sun setting above the trees, alighting the water with a ruddy glow. A darkening sky glittered with a sharp contrast of stars above shadowed pines.

"Harry?" she said. "What is this?" She heard the scrape of stools.

"This is the project Aunt Mildred became obsessed with as a child. She would walk the mudflats at low tide as a child to collect clams for dinner.

"Over time, she found pieces of pottery in the mud with her clam hook, beautiful pieces of porcelain swept downstream for hundreds of years. Soon she only went out to collect the fragments and made this mosaic. It's lovely, really."

"Amazing," Michael said. He walked back into the kitchen with Harry to finish dinner.

"Mildred, you tiny genius. What did you stumble into?" Isabelle murmured. What had caused this child to begin such an endeavor?

Isabelle surveyed it, taking it in. Nothing in the mosaic gave her a clue, and no feeling emerged other than wonder.

The sun was setting beyond the windows behind her, and she turned to see its glow cast on the river. The sky darkened above the pines, and the first star had come out. Isabelle felt she was standing between the subject and its abstract mirror image. Starting slightly with an uneasy feeling, she looked around and saw the room was empty. While she looked at the river, the hair on the back of her neck stood at attention.

Is it the river? Or the room? Isabelle thought. Had she been channeling the fear of a spirit or was it her own? The room was silent as a tomb, sounds from the kitchen gone.

Next to her, someone began to scream.

Isabelle covered her ears. It was if someone was screaming into her ear. She groaned. Plugging her ears did nothing. Scanning the room, no one emerged. Her brow furrowed in confusion.

The screaming abated to a whisper, a moan, and then silence. Slowly, she lowered her hands, untrusting. Breathing hard, Isabelle put a hand to her forehead. She recognized those screams.

Mother lay on the floor, a knife hiding its blade in her abdomen. Isabelle heard Mother screaming and came running. She hid behind the couch when she saw Father standing over her mother. He pulled the knife from Mother's body after Mom's last breath. A maniac, he smiled at Isabelle when he noticed the six-year old. That wasn't Daddy.

Sweat beaded on her forehead. Isabelle felt faint. What was causing these memories to emerge from her subconscious? She had suppressed them, hadn't thought of them in years. She had experienced the death of her mother twice upon arrival. Was a spirit using the memory to its benefit? Why had she heard her mother screaming?

Trembling, she walked back to the kitchen. Could she be losing it? Michael jumped to help her to the table when he saw her pale face.

"What happened?" Harry said. "What did you see?"

"I heard screaming," Isabelle said. "Did you?"

"No," Michael said. "You heard it in the dining room?"

She nodded. "That's why plugging my ears did nothing. It was in my head. I've heard the screams before, somewhere else. I don't know if my mind is playing tricks or if it's something here."

"Somewhere else?" Harry said.

Michael answered. "Isabelle can see spirits, and they can see her. They can see everything she has seen, her memories." He held Isabelle.

"Why would they do that?"

"One of our ideas is that some are weak; it's easier to show a memory from her life that evokes a certain emotion to convey what they want. But it makes it difficult for Isabelle to be objective at times. They stir her up."

"Lucky you," Harry said.

"Some have been waiting a long time to be heard," Isabelle said, standing on her own. Michael held her hand. "Some want to send a message to leave them be."

"Let's go to the office and turn on the listening devices," Michael said.

"Which are what?" Harry said.

"Audio recorders which capture electronic voice phenomena: EVP," Michael said. "I like to use them, although they're rarely useful."

"Apophenia," Isabelle said, shaking her head. "All it is."

"She doesn't believe in it," Michael said. "Some think we see patterns in anything we want to, and that's right to some extent. EVP can magnify background noise, including static, to the point you think you hear a spirit talking. We only include the results if something is said that Isabelle can corroborate."

Harry shivered. "You were right, I don't want to know too much. Especially since the sun is setting. Where should I be during all this? I don't want to be in your way."

"You can stay with us, go to bed, whatever you want," Michael said. "It can take a few days to pick up readings or see anything, as far as the instrumentation or my wife goes."

"Nice to be lumped in with electronics," Isabelle said.

Michael smiled.

They walked the dim hall to the office on the first floor. Harry liked that it was near the main entrance. They turned on four battery-powered lanterns to offset poor lighting and the off chance the power went out.

"Time for bed. Which rooms do you want?" Harry said.

"We brought an air mattress," Michael said. "We need to be near the computers and equipment. We camp out here." He pulled out headlamps for himself and Isabelle. Stumbling around the house in near dark was asking for an unnecessary accident, not caused by any haunting.

Five hours later, Isabelle and Michael passed coffee between them. She watched a monitor for any change in the EMF of the house, Michael for spikes in possible EVP. Sporadically, they walked the house with handheld versions of each to make sure the sensors weren't missing something in a space this large. The hallways grew longer each time, their steps slowing.

Isabelle enjoyed the full moon from each window, especially the stunning view from the back window over the yard. She wondered if the gardener too enjoyed the view before he went through the glass. Moonlight shimmered on the river and darkened the shadow of trees. It was hard to imagine anything tragic occurring here.

At midnight, Isabelle found the stairs to the attic. She whispered her intention to Michael before starting up. He remained on the third floor. The wooden steps creaked. She imagined a small girl walking them hundreds of times to create the masterpiece in the dining room. A light switch at the top revealed a large dusty room filled with old furniture covered in white linens.

Large windows at either end exposed dim outlines of treetops on the sides of the house. The lighting was poor. She stayed five minutes, sensing nothing. As she turned to walk to the staircase, dust motes stirred. A startling cloud rose from the floor.

"Hello?" Isabelle strained to hear. She saw nothing but settling dust and closed her eyes. The room temperature dropped. Isabelle shivered. Faintly, she began to hear a sound that grew in volume, a woman's voice.

"Why are you doing this? Please, stop. Stop. Stop. Stop. Stop. Stop! " The voice dissipated. Something groaned, a masculine voice. Both gone, silence returned.

The temperature rose. Nothing emerged from the shadows. Shaking, she went to the stairs and walked down, woodenly. She found Michael on the third floor.

"I know where Aunt Mildred saw a woman raped. It happened up there and explains why she became sensitive to phenomena if she played there."

"You okay, Iz?"

She nodded. He went up to test the area with the monitor and returned, shaking his head.

In a few hours, the couple would take turns sleeping. In the meantime, Harry snored softly behind them on the air mattress in the office. Isabelle smiled. He didn't last more than a half hour in his room next door before asking to stay with them. An hour after that, he was out.

"I'm surprised," Michael said. "There's hardly any background noise in the whole house, aside from his snoring."

She giggled, slaphappy. "EMF sensors are only picking up slight power surges."

Harry jumped up behind them, bellowing. His face turned beet red, the cords in his neck stood out.

"What the hell?" Michael got to his feet. "Harry, what is it? Jesus!"

Harry didn't respond. His eyes were closed, and he continued to shout. Michael looked at Isabelle for an answer, bewildered. She remembered something and slapped Harry, hard.

"What happened?" Harry's eyes snapped open.

"You tell us," Michael said, shaken. He clutched his chest, breathing hard.

Harry looked confused.

"Night terrors?" Isabelle said.

Recognition dawned on their faces.

"Really?" Michael said. "Thank goodness. I thought I had more than one medium on my hands."

Harry mumbled apologies before slumping back into bed.

At eight o'clock in the morning, Isabelle awoke. Michael lay next to her. He must have joined her when Harry left an hour before. At four a.m., she hadn't been shy about joining Harry; she needed to be near the equipment. Clattering dishes could be heard down the hall.

She stretched and got up to look at the computers. On each, she pulled up a summary chart of the past eight hours. Nothing unusual, the house was deader than a doornail thus far, aside from what happened in the attic. Not everything registered on the equipment sensors, pity, even after Michael added them to the attic.

Isabelle let Michael sleep. The hall was thankfully dark. When she reached the kitchen, the sun shriveled her retinas.

"Morning!" Harry was making eggs and toast for an army.

"Is it already?" She looked for coffee. An espresso machine was on the counter. She pointed, unbelieving.

"I'm usually stuck with instant."

Harry smiled, surprised. "I figured you were harder to please."

"I could kiss you."

Michael marched in, eyeing them. "I leave you two alone for five minutes."

"Look, honey!" Isabelle handed him her espresso.

"Can I kiss you, too?"

Harry laughed. "We can all kiss my butler when this is over." He handed out plates of eggs.

Over the course of the day, Isabelle sat in different rooms, taking notes. She wrote about anything that caught her eye. She paid attention with her senses but felt nothing odd. Michael poured over research Harry had gleaned about the property.

Michael joined Isabelle when she reached the pool on the first floor in the afternoon. She had worked down from the attic, choosing the poolroom last, considering her drowning vision in the car. She sat in a brass chair aged lime and looked across the smooth water of the twenty-five yard pool.

A wall of windows over half the pool jutted onto the majestic lawn. Shrubbery and the river beyond were visible. Some of the windows had clinging condensation from the chlorine-scented water below.

Michael sat next to her and sighed. "Anything?"

"I'm wondering if what happened here affected me before we arrived. On the drive here, I experienced the sensation of being underwater. I couldn't see when I opened my eyes."

"I knew something happened. Why didn't you tell—"

"Michael, Harry was blabbering on like a horse's ass. Anyway, I couldn't see, meaning the water had to be dark. Maybe the room wasn't lit when somebody drowned?"

"That makes sense if it was in the 1800s," Michael said. "Only had candles at the time. The original sconces are on the walls. Drowned at night?"

"The pool had to have been different then, replaced by this modern one."

Something moved in the background over Michael's shoulder. A dark head of hair lifted out of the water.

"Isabelle, are you all right?" Michael reached for her hand.

She managed a hushed whisper. "Something is communicating."

A figure shrouded in white walked up the steps, slow and deliberate, back to them on the far side of the pool. A small and unimposing figure finally turned, and Isabelle saw a little girl. The shroud was a white dress, soaked wet. Brown hair hung in strings. A white face and hands held a blue cast, lips a dark purple.

Isabelle grasped the arms of the chair. The girl continued at an agonizing pace. Michael quieted, looking for signs where Isabelle gazed. Isabelle's eyes traced a path to where they sat. Michael sat up straight. The girl came to stand next to the coffee table between their facing chairs.

"Isabelle, can you help me?" said the girl, voice distant. "I don't want to stay here." The child appeared tired, exerted from getting out of the pool.

"I might be able to. What is your name?" Isabelle felt empathy for all tortured spirits, especially children.

"Constance."

"Okay, thank you. Did the woman who took care of you…hurt you, Constance?"

"No, my nanny loved me as if I were her own." The child looked around, startled.

"Do you know who did hurt you? Or could you not swim?"

"I can swim, really well. I don't know her name." She shuddered, clearly afraid.

"A lady hurt you? How do you know it was a lady?"

"She wore a long red dress," Constance said. "I was admiring it when she threw me in."

"I'm sorry she hurt you," Isabelle said. "I would have admired a dress like that, too."

"You can see it when she comes out again," Constance said. "She still wears it."

Isabelle sat up straighter, uncomfortable in the hard chair. "Is she here with you?"

"Stay away from her, if you can. Please, don't let me stay in the water forever." The girl turned and walked a slow path to the water. Halting staccato steps, as if willing each foot to go before the other, she gave Isabelle a poignant stare as she disappeared below the surface.

Isabelle shivered in the warm, humid room. Michael raised his eyebrows.

"The girl who drowned, Constance Smith." He looked at the water.

"Her nanny was Eleanor Bridges. It was ruled accidental; the nanny thought the child was at the party, but Constance came here. They found the girl under the pool cover. She said a woman did kill her?"

"A woman in a red dress. According to Constance, I can see her wearing it."

Michael sucked in a breath.

"Yes, we may have a class five on our hands."

⁖ ⁖ ⁖

They filled Harry in with details of the poolroom encounter as he drank coffee in the kitchen.

"My God, that little girl is trapped here? Why?"

"I think we will find out," Isabelle said.

"Did you find records on the man who fell down the stairs?" Michael said.

Harry had made a call to town hall that afternoon. "I retrieved a death certificate, that's all. The examiner ruled it accidental. The man was a business partner and close friend of my great grandfather. His name was William Geraldine. My great grandfather was hosting a party where they celebrated the purchase of a small company.

"I have thought about it, and the only staircase people would take from a ball or any sort of celebration would have to be the grand staircase. The ballroom is on the second floor along with the smoking room and several meeting rooms," Harry said. "William was drunk at time of death, according to the report."

"I will keep an eye on the staircase," Isabelle said.

Afternoon melted into dusk. Dinner arrived with filet mignon, potatoes, and corn.

"You'd think we were on vacation," Isabelle said, eagerly accepting her plate.

"At least taste this local microbrew with it," Harry said and handed her a brown bottle. "No argument."

Isabelle sighed.

"Thank you. It's very good, Harry," Michael said. He glanced sidelong at Isabelle. "So far the energy here seems tame. Go for it, hon."

"About as tame as a coiled rattlesnake," Isabelle said. "But I'll give it a taste. Famous last words."

"You've got us to protect you," Harry said. "And there's always the door. Sleep on the lawn. What's a ghost going to do? Now, raise your bottles."

One beer turned into three each as they talked and laughed. Isabelle and Michael didn't have many friends, and they welcomed the camaraderie. Isabelle felt good for the first time in days. The assignment at hand seemed hardly to matter. Harry was telling story after story that had them in stitches.

"You wouldn't believe the school uniforms!" Harry said, pounding the counter. "It was rumored that my gym teacher was gay, and my mother proved it when she shrunk my shorts and refused to buy me more. He made me scale the rope an extra five times that gym class!"

Isabelle and Michael almost tipped off their bar stools in hysterics. The room dimmed and brightened too much for a power surge.

Great, Isabelle, fall down drunk on the job, she thought. Then she saw the woman behind Harry.

A complete stranger stood in the corner of the kitchen, staring at *her*. Isabelle's pulse quickened. Dark hair contrasted with the pallor of skin. She wore a dark red, velvet sleeveless gown. Her hair was pulled up, glamorous. Dark circles under her eyes told a different story; a young woman in her mid-twenties, too young to be dead.

Staring at them with disapproval, eyes dark, intense. Stunned, Isabelle had never seen a spirit appear so solid. She looked alive as the three of them. Harry and Michael didn't notice, didn't see. The woman wore a necklace. She had never seen a spirit wear jewelry either. Isabelle made out a beautiful white jewel on the woman's bosom.

The eyes didn't wander. Isabelle felt the energy in the room change. It felt charged, uncomfortable, and it was building.

An alarm went off in the office. Michael and Harry jumped up and ran to it. She wanted to yell at them but couldn't breathe, let alone speak. Isabelle was alone but not really.

Don't be a fool, Isabelle, she thought. *Say something.* She closed her eyes, dreading even a moment when she couldn't see this spirit but needing some composure nonetheless. Opening her eyes, finding her words.

"I am Isabelle. I am a friend. I do not wish you harm, only to make contact and learn from your life." She stammered. The woman didn't move or bat an eye. Nothing to indicate she heard Isabelle.

Isabelle looked to see if Michael was coming down the hall. Seeing nothing, she turned back. The woman was inches away. Brown eyes searing, pale skin close enough to see pores. A white hand lunged and clasped Isabelle by the throat.

Unbelieving, Isabelle cried out as the spirit knocked her to the floor, stool clattering on the tile. The cold hand had monstrous strength. Isabelle's vision clouded. Somewhere she heard Michael cry out. Isabelle thought the torment would stop with his arrival. It didn't.

Isabelle found Michael's terrified face over the shoulder of the leering woman. Isabelle mouthed a word. He nodded and retrieved a butcher knife from a magnetized wall strip. He ran back and thrust it into her hand, blade up. The spirit sneered, inches from Isabelle's blue-tinged face.

She stabbed the spirit. The woman let go, dropping Isabelle, clutching her chest. The knife fell. Isabelle sucked in breaths of molten air that burned on the way down. The woman gaped at her unwounded chest. She leapt up, furious.

Isabelle swore as she stood with Michael's help.

"What the hell is going on?" Harry said.

"You okay?" Michael said. "What happened?"

Horrified, Isabelle watched as the woman picked the knife from the floor. The apparition walked by her, gown swishing. Those eyes focused on Harry then Isabelle then Harry, goading her.

"Run, Harry!" Isabelle yelled, her voice box finally working.

"Why?" He said, stepping back. The woman was a foot from him. *Didn't he see the knife?*

"Just do it!" Michael said. Harry turned and fled, his skin marble white. Isabelle blinked when she saw the woman run after him.

"Oh my God," Isabelle ran, too. Michael followed.

"What is it, dammit?" he said, out of breath as they turned right and ran down the main hall through the center of the house.

"The woman in the red dress!"

As they neared the front door, Isabelle heard Harry pound up the grand staircase.

They entered the foyer, and she saw the ghost follow him up the stairs, mere feet behind. They ran up the stairs and fled down the hall to a dead end. Isabelle and Michael fell into a large ballroom with walls entirely covered in gilded mirrors. Isabelle saw the woman stand over him as Harry doubled over to breathe, her face reflected at infinitesimal angles around them.

The woman raised a hand, aiming the knife above the middle of Harry's back. Isabelle screamed. The knife plunged, blood flowering his white shirt. He crumbled. Isabelle lunged toward Harry, but Michael grabbed her shoulders. Something clattered to the floor.

The woman smiled, taunting Isabelle. Michael turned his wife around and slapped her as hard as he dared. Isabelle stared, unbelieving.

"What is wrong with her?" Harry said.

She saw Harry standing in the middle of the room. She looked back to Michael. Swallowing, she put a hand to her mouth. The woman was gone. Then she saw the knife. It was behind Michael, near the door.

Tears welling in her eyes, Isabelle pointed to the knife, questioning. Michael nodded.

"You dropped it a second ago, honey," he said, his voice thick with fear. "What happened?"

Isabelle took a deep breath that wanted to become panic. She leaned over, hands on knees, head down to offset dizziness.

"Jesus." Harry was at her side in an instant. They each grabbed an arm.

"Class five poltergeist," Isabelle heaved. "Unless I imagined it. Am I going crazy?"

"Unless we're imagining that handprint around your neck," Harry said, "you're perfectly sane."

Dusk had deepened into night. They found a stone bench on the front lawn. Michael rubbed her back as Isabelle gave every detail. Harry trembled when she told the last of the story and realized the implication. Michael rubbed his temples.

"What did you see?" Isabelle said.

"Nothing out of the ordinary," Michael said. Harry nodded in agreement.

"Did you see the knife when she picked it up?"

"No, you carried the knife from the kitchen upstairs," Michael said.

"How did I see her holding it?" Isabelle felt sick. The men shook their heads.

"Why did you want it?" Harry said.

"A theory of mine. Basically, poltergeists of this magnitude can't accept they are dead. I reminded her, and she didn't like it."

"Reverse psychology for the dead," Michael said, both amused and grim.

"Why did she go after *me*, then?" Harry said.

"Good question." Isabelle stared at the grass, black as the sky now. "I saw her stab you, blood soaked your shirt, and you were on the floor. How did I see her kill you?"

"I don't know, Isabelle. This is a first, right?" Michael said.

"She's very strong. She choked me hard enough to leave a mark. How have we not known she was here this entire time?"

"The woman who went missing, what was her name and what year did she disappear?" Michael said.

"1816," Harry said. "Her name was Genevieve Milton."

"The spirit was wearing a gown," Isabelle said.

"Fit for a ball in the 19th century?" Michael said.

"Definitely. That would make her almost two hundred years dead."

"Miss Milton is notorious for ruining the first gala my great great grandfather had here, four years after the house was built. Town records show a search party was sent out the day following the event and in subsequent weeks."

"Isabelle, I'm not sure I want to go back in there," Michael said, shaken. "I can't wait to document what you've seen; I never thought it possible. But this spirit worked you like a puppeteer. What else can she do to us? It's not worth it."

"I can see her. I can keep us safe," Isabelle said. "This is the end-all job for our work. She didn't hurt Harry! Just sent a message to me, to all of us." She added on the latter, covering the sneaking suspicion the message was indeed meant for her. Isabelle had used the knife to trick the spirit into letting go. The infamous Miss Milton had then taught Isabelle a lesson.

"She hurt you," Michael said. "We have enough for our research."

"We must finish the job!"

"Look, you confirmed my aunt wasn't trying to rob me of my childhood. You saw something real. You don't have to go back in there," Harry said.

"Harry, don't you want to know how she died, only to remain in this house? There is a reason she can't find absolution. Michael, did anything show on EMF?"

"There was a strong plateau in pulse. I didn't realize why it was a plateau until now. It stayed at a high level while you were attacked and then dropped. I've never seen electromagnetivity of this magnitude."

"I felt it," Isabelle said. "In the kitchen, I felt the field build around her before the alarm went off."

"We should never have left you," Michael said.

"It didn't matter if you were by me. She's willing to chase us all over the house!"

"Right, so how about we leave and stay in a hotel until the morning and have my staff come back for your equipment?" Harry offered.

Isabelle got up, disgusted, and, to their astonishment, walked back into the orange maw of the house.

"Why are we back inside?" Harry yelled from the doorway as Michael stormed past him. "I'm not paying you enough for this!"

Harry took a look around before shutting the door and followed Michael. They found her in the office.

"Isabelle!" Michael said. "Are you insane? You think you can keep us all safe?" Michael shook his head.

"This will lead to answers, Michael," Isabelle said. "We have to write about a class five. We know almost nothing!" Her throat hurt. Unconsciously, she rubbed the bruise.

"She toyed with you, a professional medium. You've dealt with spirits all your life."

"We need to learn from this," Isabelle said, desperately.

"You're not thinking clearly. You're getting greedy in your career. Maybe this spirit is getting to you."

"Something happened in my childhood to initiate my interaction with the dead. Something with my father and mother. Starting with the drive here, I have felt a connection between this place and that moment. I don't know what it is, but I intend to find out."

Michael swallowed. He knew her mother had died when she was young, but they never discussed details. Isabelle refused. He knew the argument was over.

"I would like answers, too," Harry whispered. "I'm tired of wondering what happened here and conjuring up answers in my nightmares."

"Guess I'm outnumbered," Michael said, grumbling. "We all stay together. Let's get going and scan the house. Isabelle, attach the recording device."

They entered the hall. Michael checked the sensors while Isabelle and Harry peered at the handheld EMF. They each had a flashlight in the dimmed house lights. It was an eerie feeling; every time Isabelle shined the light into the shadows, she expected to see the woman lunge for her.

Keep breathing, she thought. In these types of situations, she told herself spirits were trying to tell their story. She didn't know if that logic would fit here, however.

On the landing in front of the great window, they faced the dark river below, stars caught in its surface. It was the same sight Isabelle admired the night before. She felt a cold chill instead of awe. The window reflected their flashlights, and movement caught her eye. She saw the silhouette of a woman in a dress next to herself.

Gasping, Isabelle shined the light to her right. Nothing.

"What?" Michael cried out.

"Let's leave the landing," she said. "Grab the railing!" If this spirit was responsible for the gardener's demise, she didn't want to be part of the reenactment.

The guys swore but followed orders. Isabelle grasped the railing with all her strength. They each rotated their light in all directions. Isabelle expected a cold hand to clutch her throat. They left the landing, slowly, while gripping the banister, and ran toward the grand staircase. The hallway before them seemed eternal. Isabelle felt a sense of dread and pushed it aside. An alarm went off downstairs.

"Wish I was down there to know where the hell this thing is!" Michael said. Isabelle was behind Harry, and his light illuminated a picture-sized mirror on the wall to her right in a brief flash. It was long enough to reveal the woman and her white face, teeth bared.

"Faces in the glass," Isabelle said.

"What?" Michael said.

"Saw her in the mirror," Isabelle said.

Harry whimpered. Claws of fear tore at Isabelle. She held onto the rail as they jogged down the grand staircase. Halfway down, something pulled the back of her shirt, a gentle tug, but Isabelle screamed and lost her footing.

I'm falling, she thought, too fast to cry out a warning. Isabelle piled into Harry and drove him face first into Michael, who screamed in surprise. Isabelle felt a final moment of sickening free-fall before they thudded to a stop at the base of the steps. Laughter echoed in the foyer.

"Are you all right?" Michael asked.

Isabelle did a self-check, noting Harry's elbow in her left eye socket, a headache behind that eye. Harry mumbled a yes from below.

"Good, then get off me," Michael said with strain. They all stood after gingerly untangling.

"We leaving?" Harry was panting, and the flashlight shook in his hand, creating a staccato light trail on the marble. Isabelle would have said yes, but she saw something in the beam that made her pause. Light trembled on a painting of water winding through a sunlit countryside at the entrance of the foyer. It was moving.

Isabelle walked toward it, head cocked. She heard Michael utter obscenities but then he obviously saw it, too. The picture frame wasn't moving, which would have been somewhat normal. No, the water was flowing, currents visible as it bubbled over rocks in a field of tall grass.

"Pictures that move," Isabelle said. "I bet your aunt saw this every day, Harry."

"Holy shit," Harry whispered. "Everything was true? She grew up here, in this hell hole." He shook with terror. Isabelle held his hand, sympathetic.

"Harry and I are starting to see paranormal evidence," Michael said into a recording device.

Something glimmered in her peripheral vision. Shining her light, Isabelle saw the white walls rippling. She gasped when she saw three people in the doorway. Constance Smith held the hands of a man in coveralls, another man in a suit next to them. The little girl met Isabelle's eyes. Harry dropped his light with a clatter.

"She killed us," Constance said, crying.

"That's the gardener, John. And there's…William, my great grandfather's business partner," Harry said, incredulous. "I know him from a photograph."

"The one who died on the stairs?" Michael asked.

Harry nodded.

Isabelle knelt before the girl. "Why did she kill you?"

"Go to the river," Constance said. "Find her grave."

"Who, Constance? Genevieve?" Isabelle pressed, but Constance backed away with the others. They grew faint as they passed into darkness, but Isabelle saw the girl give a small nod.

Isabelle found her way back to the office, shaking with what everything could mean. It was Genevieve Milton. She had killed those poor souls. What ghost could entrap even one spirit? They had never documented a being so powerful. Isabelle realized she didn't know if she could keep them all safe. Was she being careless? Michael and Harry followed, happy to be back in the well-lit room.

"There are no paintings, no mirrors, and no knives here," Isabelle said. "We'll be okay. We can figure this out and get this bitch back where she belongs."

"What does 'Go to the river' mean?" Michael said.

"The mural your aunt made," Isabelle said. "It's of the river. The painting with flowing water. It's all a message. Genevieve is communicating her death."

"They would have found a body downstream," Harry said. "First place they would have looked. They drag the river bottom for bodies to this day."

"'Find her grave,'" Isabelle said. "Constance didn't say the river was her grave."

A woman screamed upstairs, far overhead. The attic. The screams were different from last night, when she heard her mother. Isabelle ran toward them. They pounded up the back stairs to the attic.

They discovered the room decorated in 19th century furniture, the linens gone. Isabelle recognized the shrill cries coming from a dark corner. She had heard them the first night when she was here alone.

Walking together, they passed a large wardrobe, and as they rounded it, caught view of the man. His back to them, he wore dark pants and a white shirt, sleeves rolled up. He was holding the arms of a woman on the divan, pinning her. Isabelle couldn't see the woman but saw the edge of a red velvet dress. He groaned with pleasure as the woman gave a feeble cry, sobbing. The man straightened and fixed his clothes. Isabelle heard the woman asking why.

He lifted her in his arms and turned toward the three. Harry sucked in a breath as light showed their faces.

"My great great grandfather, Arnaud," he said. "My heritage." Isabelle barely recognized Genevieve. She didn't look angry. Instead, she was haggard-faced, hair torn, and limp in his arms.

Arnaud LaFleur stalked past with her, and they followed him down the stairs, through the house and poolroom, out onto the lawn. Genevieve began to scream as they neared the edge of the river. LaFleur was swift. He threw her into the shallow water from the rocky edge and waded in.

She resurfaced and screamed in pain from hitting rocks. He gave her no time to regain herself. He pushed her chest and head under water. Her arms and legs flailed for an agonizing minute then stilled.

Genevieve floated to the surface. LaFleur looked around and saw the water wasn't flowing. It was stagnant, halfway between low and full tide. His crime of passion hadn't been premeditated.

"What is he going to do?" Isabelle said. Looking at the house, all lights were on and loud voices carried from the ballroom in 1816. "He should have been caught."

LaFleur responded as if in answer to Isabelle and dragged the body out of the water. He laid Genevieve on the lawn and made for a gardening shed. Harry and Michael looked at each other.

LaFleur grabbed a shovel and started digging near the shed, under trees with low branches. Sounds made by LaFleur began to dissipate as he faded from sight. Lights dimmed and laughter faded to silence in the house.

"Time to go back in," Isabelle said. The sun rose over the trees with dawn, and they all felt relief, though Isabelle and Michael knew it meant little protection.

Isabelle walked with firm resolution to the dining room. She turned to the mosaic. Something glinted in her peripheral vision. Turning, she saw the butcher knife on the table. *How did it get there?*

Genevieve is toying with me, she thought. Looking around, no one was there. Isabelle walked closer to the mosaic. She had to figure this out, fast. Harry entered with Michael.

"The knife," Harry said. "How?"

"Do you really need to ask?" Michael said.

Isabelle ignored them. "Why did Mildred have this obsession? Why the pottery from the river?"

She saw a white piece in the river. Odd, there weren't any other white fragments in the river. It was rounded, unlike the others. She pulled up a chair to stand on and leaned in to observe a large white opal jewel, four fish etched into its surface. They swam in a tight circle, nose to tail. Isabelle smiled.

"What is it?" Harry said.

"The necklace Genevieve wore when she died," Isabelle said. "Minus the chain. Aunt Mildred found her necklace, and all the baggage that came with it." She pointed out the two hundred-year old opal gemstone.

Turning around, Isabelle almost fell off the chair when she saw Genevieve behind Harry.

"It was given to me by my fiancé, the man I loved," Genevieve said. The ethereal voice resonated through the walls. Harry and

Michael jumped at the sound, eyes wide. They turned and *saw* with jaw-dropping clarity the beauty among them.

"The stone shows the eternity meant for us." Sadness crept into her voice.

"You can't be with him?" Isabelle said, stepping gingerly off the chair.

"What Arnaud did to me that night…he stole my love from me, the promise made by my fiancé. I have tried to leave, but Arnaud made that impossible. His power holds me prisoner. I believe that's why you're here."

Isabelle let out a sigh of relief. "We do want to help."

"You already have. Arnaud's brood is once again in the house. Thank you."

Harry gasped, white as a sheet.

"Harry isn't the same man as Arnaud," Isabelle said. "I won't let you hurt him. You need to find another resolution."

"He carries the same blood and same sin," the spirit hissed. "He must pay. After I died, all I was capable of was a push here, a little force there. Otherwise I would have killed Arnaud. Constance, she was easy to lure, an easy kill. Arnaud realized then that I wanted him and left the house. I couldn't follow." Disappointment imbedded her voice.

"Why did you kill that little girl?" Isabelle cried. "And William? The gardener? What did they do?"

"The girl was a member of Arnaud's family," Genevieve said, coldly. "I could feel his blood in her veins. Her death gave me strength. The others were of no importance; they were tests. Now I can stand before you." She turned her steel gaze on Harry.

"Arnaud's power fills you, Harry," Genevieve said. "His eyes look through yours."

"I'm sorry for what he did to you," Harry said, softly. "It was monstrous, unspeakable. I'm ashamed to be related."

"If apologies were enough," Genevieve said. "I wouldn't be here."

"They can be enough," Isabelle said. "I won't let you kill him."

"Who says I will be the one to do it?" Genevieve thrust her chin, defiant.

Isabelle looked at her, questioning. She looked into Genevieve's liquid brown eyes. A flash of light filled her mind. Isabelle saw her father, his insane grin. It was her torturous memory again. The image of her father faded, and she saw a different man. A stranger with scraggly black hair and beard stubble stood over her mother, leering. He wore patched and ripped clothing, filthy, a drifter.

The memory replayed, and Isabelle watched as the drifter killed her mother as her father had. He grinned at Isabelle as her father did. When her mother gave her last breath, the man stood and smiled sweetly as he cut the throat of her father.

No," Isabelle said, snapping from the vision. "No, no, no! This isn't real! My father killed my mother. I don't know why you're showing me this. I saw everything."

Genevieve smiled, enigmatic and beautiful. "You saw what your mind told you to see. Ever since that moment, you have seen the dead. Why can you see me? Your father embodied that spirit because he was weak, allowing a psychotic wanting one more kill to possess him."

"No." Isabelle shook her head, vehement.

"No? You refuse to remember. From your memory, I have gleaned there are others like me with such strength. I can do more than throw men through windows."

Another flash of light, and Isabelle picked up the knife. She could feel Genevieve crawl through her mind, control her fingertips. Hatred poured into her heart. In three strides she gripped Harry LaFleur and thrust the knife into his heart.

Michael shook her out of the trance, where she stood near the mosaic, far from the knife.

"Harry!" Gasping, Isabelle collapsed.

"I'm all right," Harry said, kneeling by her with Michael. Genevieve remained on the other side of the table.

Isabelle started to cry. She had felt the knife when it slid into Harry. Horrified at the perverse satisfaction she felt, even knowing it wasn't her own. Genevieve clung to Isabelle like an unwanted residue.

"My God," Isabelle said. "I was too young to understand. All this time, I've been afraid of meeting someone like you again."

Michael gave Isabelle an encouraging nod. Harry was shaking. They were running out of time.

Isabelle felt Genevieve try to lure her into another trance. If she gave up her mind to Genevieve, she wouldn't come out of it until Harry was dead.

Isabelle jumped onto the chair to get the white opal. After two hard pulls, she yanked it off the mosaic. Genevieve clutched for her necklace as it disappeared from her neck.

"I believe this does represent eternity," Isabelle said. Genevieve darted toward her, sliding over the floor in an effortless blur.

"Isabelle, you don't have much time!" Michael said.

Isabelle threw the opal onto the floor. Genevieve reached her, took her arm. Tottering, Isabelle fell off the chair, and, at first, her foot found nothing but empty marble. Then she saw the opal, and before Genevieve could drag her away, her shoe heel smashed at the piece, breaking it into fragments.

"What have you done?" Genevieve screamed. She grabbed Isabelle's face, fingernails peeling flesh.

"You had a little girl bring your necklace into the house to keep it safe," Isabelle said, sneering. "To protect you. You could have been free but you chose to stay!"

Genevieve grew weak. She pulled away, her form fading.

"How will I find my love? You have destroyed everything!"

"I'm sorry for what happened to you," Isabelle said. "But after what you've done, you may not deserve that love." The woman watched Isabelle, eyes mournful as the last of her red velvet dress slipped into the ether.

They heard a little girl laugh and turned to see Constance skip around the room. She, too, was fading. Others began to pour in, men and women of all ages and dress; they entered from the walls and looked at Isabelle and smiled or laughed before disappearing.

"How did you know what to do?" Michael asked as she and Harry sat outside in the sun. "I was at a loss!"

Isabelle sighed. "I guessed. Genevieve followed the necklace into the house with Aunt Mildred, therefore she needed to have it nearby.

I knew when I first saw her that she placed too much hold in the physical. She walked like us. I stabbed her with a knife, and she thought herself wounded. As she became more powerful, she felt alive again."

She told them about the visions the ghost had shown her, and, for the first time, described to Michael what happened to her parents.

"I don't know if it needs to be said, but thank you for not stabbing me," Harry said, hugging Isabelle. She shook him off with a chuckle. "How did you know she had a choice when she died? She made it sound like her death made her a prisoner."

"I will tell you one thing about death," Isabelle said. "We always get a choice. To stay or move on, no matter how we die. Don't stay for revenge, don't stay for anything."

Michael looked as surprised as Harry at the revelation.

"I'm sorry you ever had to witness such a horrific event as a child, let alone that it happened to your parents." Michael was grim. Isabelle, however, felt relief for the first time since she was six years old. Her father hadn't been a murderer. He hadn't been crazy. He hadn't killed her mother senselessly.

"It's unfortunate what happened to Genevieve, but she made it worse by spreading evil. However, she did something I am grateful for." Isabelle smiled.

"What's that, Iz?"

"Cleared my father's name."

About the Author

Michelle K. Bujnowski has been writing short horror fiction for over a decade while working as a geologist throughout the country. She currently stays at home with her high-energy 21-month old, Ethan, and she and her husband Tom look forward to the arrival of his baby brother in March. Michelle has published with *The Literary Hatchet, Dark Moon Digest, The Lightning Journal,* and *Dark Edifice Magazine.*

TWICE PER ANNUM

Aaron Vlek

I

Twice per annum, Elwood Addington Thrush engaged in what he called his Grande Purge. On April 23rd and November 16th, dates chosen for obscure reasons kept strictly to himself, various things among the accumulated flotsam of his cluttered existence would be meticulously exhumed from the farthest reaches of his closets and drawers and extricated with an almost surgical precision from the deepest recesses of the attic and basement.

All would then be gathered together into a great pile in the middle of his vast living room: piles of luggage and mountains of clothes, boxes and bags all thrown on the pile, books and trinkets as well as a thousand small mementos of a life, of his life, alone and solitary. These would be considered silently for one hour, no more, no less. During this time, nothing would be touched, handled, or reflected upon in its own particularity.

After this hour of considered reflection had expired, the nature and contents of which he never disclosed to anyone nor wrote down the least report, the pile would be unsentimentally consigned to a huge industrial waste bin Thrush rented from a local contractor and had placed discretely toward the back of his modest acreage. All would then be carted away to an undisclosed destination. This purge typically, and in some quarters notoriously, included not only objects both priceless and common but extended without mercy to persons as well, and included both those occupying the outer fringes of his minor acquaintance, as well as those placed much closer to the seat of his most intimate and private affairs.

It came then as absolutely no surprise to Fredreich and Mathilde-Eloise when Thrush left detailed instructions on the ancient salver outside their quarters the night of November 15th charging them to lay another place setting at the table in the formal dining room for breakfast the next morning. They were to spare no effort or expense in the preparation of the early morning repast, to be taken just after first light, behind closed doors, with no interruptions of any sort to be tolerated for any reason short of imminent loss of life or limb to either themselves or the portly canine companion of advanced age who shared the Thrush household. What did come as something of a shock to the elderly pair, long used to a diverse and unpredictable assemblage of eccentricities of manner and taste in their employer, was the guest's identity: Thrush's daughter, Violette Marie Constance, a person the elder Thrush had not seen, nor had any sort of contact with, for over forty years.

Fredreich and Mathilde-Eloise were in the kitchen when the doorbell finally emitted its solitary sonorous note that vibrated throughout the entire house and into the farthest wings of the massive structure. Mattie, as Fredreich referred to his wife privately and out of hearing range of their employer, shot a pensive glance at her husband, and he returned her gaze, holding it for a full ten seconds before releasing it as he set the silver tray with its formal service back onto the marble counter top. Mathilde-Eloise wiped her hands nervously on her linen apron and glanced toward the front of the house but said nothing, merely illustrating the tone of the moment with a sharp involuntary intake of breath.

After straightening his crisp jacket and tugging the points snuggly into place—pressed flat and centered against his narrow, wiry frame—Fredreich glided silently, and with a dignity seldom witnessed outside the Thrush residence, toward the entry hall where he pulled open the massive ornamental iron door to receive the guest. Stepping back against the interior flank of the stone entry way and assuming a stiffened attitude of attention, eyes locked straight ahead and not looking directly at the woman herself, Fredreich awaited further instructions or developments.

Violette Marie Constance Thrush nodded once sharply, whether to Fredreich as a sort of greeting or to the house itself for unknown reasons remained unclear. She stepped over the ancient mosaic threshold as the first rays of misty predawn penetrated the stained glass windows in the foyer. She paused there for a moment before carefully removing her calf-length camel hair cape, suede gloves of the same precise hue, and green felt hunter's hat, complete with two crisp pheasant plumes more than sixteen inches in length, then wordlessly draped them over Fredreich's waiting arm. Then she pulled off her dark glasses and proceeded to examine the entry hall, her knuckled index finger tapping thoughtfully against her pursed lips. Eyes narrowed and beady, she raked with extreme care over every surface and detail within view.

"Something is different," she said slowly, not glancing at Fredreich, but continuing her studied consideration of each surface, object, and architectural detail, drawing from a long faded memory of the place and attempting to understand the current vision with an adult's eye, for the very first time.

"A great deal, Miss Thrush," came a hollow yet musical voice from the adjoining Turkish salon, "has changed." The senior Thrush stepped lightly into view from behind the faded rose velvet draperies and beheld his daughter with his usual guarded demeanor, hands clasped firmly before him just below the waist. His great height and lean, unstooped frame remained as imposing in command as when last they'd met, in this very house, so many decades ago and under circumstances not disposed to inspire fond memories and the warmest of reunions.

"This way, please," Thrush said curtly, stepping aside as he and Violette Marie Constance disappeared into the vast spaces of the formal dining room where the massive chandelier and numerous ornate sconces had been set alight, illuminating the ancient walls and carved ceiling with a flickering, buttery glow.

"Fredreich, I believe we're ready to be served now," Thrush instructed as he closed the massive carved double doors behind him, sealing himself and his final surviving offspring into familial privacy before the dusty imperviousness of the family crest where it commanded a place of prominence some ten feet above over the mantle of the fireplace.

"Very good, sir," whispered the manservant as he turned and went to rejoin his wife in the kitchen.

II

It was Christmas Eve, some forty years prior to the events of the somewhat reserved reunion between Thrush and his daughter Violette Marie Constance on the morning of November 16th. Alas, but the stockings were not hung by the chimney with care, and St. Nick—long considered by Thrush to be a wholly frivolous encumbrance on the critical formative years of childhood—had been summarily banished to the abodes of lesser children in the neighborhood.

To the mind of Elwood Addington Thrush, his progeny were to be more suitably occupied and consumed by matters of undeniable intellectual gravity and import such as a close study of the Classics, the venerable arts of antiquity and the Renaissance, and preparation for productive livelihoods in law, medicine, the Academy, and needless to state, the continuation of the Thrush family name. This last was to be achieved with the assistance of suitable youth to be carefully selected by Thrush and certain of his confederates among the Old Garde of his Club.

But on this particular Christmas Eve, the Thrush family would dine modestly in the smaller dining room on lamb with shallots and white wine and various hardy accompaniments as Mathilde-Eloise found on hand in the pantry. She had purchased at her own personal expense a number of pine garlands and arranged them attractively over the small white marble fireplace, and Fredreich had brought candy and a few small gifts for the children. Thrush had looked upon these displays and grunted approvingly, but had said nothing. He had done his duty to the season by placing generous yearly envelopes on the salver outside the door to his servants' quarters.

As for the children and Felicity, his wife, Thrush had provided a hearty meal, prepared by the best staff his robust resources could afford, and Fredreich would be driving them to church at the end of the evening. Tomorrow was another day. They would eat the remains of this meal or the offerings of another, the heady pine scent of Mathilde's garlands would amuse the children, and then they would move swiftly and with purpose toward the New Year.

As they sat together in the grand salon waiting for Fredreich to call them in to dinner, Felicity stood at the window, admiring her favorite sight: the unobstructed view of the Hudson River on its silent march toward the waiting arms of Manhattan and the sea beyond. Three of Elwood and Felicity's four daughters, Amelia Cecile, Violette Marie Constance, and Daphne Alice, sat before the roaring fire playing Whist—a game much favored by the Thrush women—and eying the box of confections sitting on the table that had been strictly designated for after dinner only.

The snow had begun to fall earlier in the day and now lay as a three-foot thick blanket over the rose garden and the walking path, while the tree branches sagged heavily under its powdery weight. This had put Felicity into a festive mood that utterly baffled and clearly irked her husband.

"My dearest, why on this earth would you rejoice in something that only makes for dreary and dangerous work for our Fredreich? It's highly unthinking of you, and I hope you will refrain from such childish displays in the future or confine this silliness to the children's rooms," Thrush admonished, glancing at Felicity and shaking his head as she continued to gaze at the river.

"You could at least look at your husband when he speaks to you in such a tone. It reflects poorly on my authority," he grumbled.

"No one questions your authority in this house, my dear Thrush," she began lightly, turning to look at him and coming to sit at his side on the divan.

"It is well known and thoroughly understood," she continued, patting his arm affectionately. "Now, would it be possible, do you think, for Fredreich to drive our girls and me up Route 9 to look at the snow and, well, the houses? You know, I love seeing how people decorate at this time of year," she asked hopefully.

"Yes, certainly," Thrush replied, happy for the occasion to bestow permission where he suspected more and more that none was truly required.

"And perhaps Mathilde-Eloise, might she go as well?"

"Oh yes, please!" the girls cried out happily.

"If the house is in proper order," Thrush replied sternly. "And Fredreich does not require some task of her in the kitchens, and you are away for no more than two hours, then yes," he concluded firmly, glaring at them as though they had all gone mad. "And where is Augusta Clarice? Call her. We'll be dining shortly, and I don't want to be seated at the table waiting for her, again. It happens with altogether far too much frequency, and I want it stopped," Thrush said angrily as the three other girls got up and ran from the room in search of their sister.

Just a few moments later, the service bell rang outside the salon door, and Thrush stood up, believing it to be the call that dinner could be served at the family's leisure. Instead, after the customary count to ten, the door swung open, and Fredreich entered and walked up to where Thrush stood.

"A word, sir, if I might," Fredreich said in a hushed tone while gesturing toward the door.

"Yes, yes, Fredreich, we'll dine now, as soon as my daughter deems us worthy of her company. Her siblings are even now in search of her."

"Sir, a word, if you please," the manservant said curtly, his eyes stark with such fanatic emotion that Thrush, startled, glanced at his wife and then followed Fredreich out the door without a word.

"What is it, man?" Thrush demanded, his face a mask of anger and confusion. "Out with it, if…" His words trailed off as he saw the tear welling up in Fredreich's eye.

"Come," Fredreich whispered hoarsely and then quickly lead the way to the mezzanine observatory above the second floor where the wooden and metal door, like that of a fortress vault, stood ajar, and one of the great door-sized windows beyond lay wide open, allowing the icy winds to violently tear at the draperies and already leaving a considerable pile of snow on the floor beneath.

"I just came up here to check the door, sir. I felt the cold air and realized the window was open so I, naturally I, sir…she had already fallen before I got here. Look, sir," Fredreich choked. "See there, she's almost completely covered with snow. She could not have survived such a fall from this height, sir. I'm so sorry. We must go down and get her," he continued, tugging gently at Thrush's coat sleeve where he stood immobile, staring down at the small form of his youngest child, twelve-year-old Augusta Clarice, her body broken and lying at a horrible angle far below.

"How?" Thrush gasped and visibly staggered. "I don't understand." Then he heard the scream of his wife behind him as she clung violently to his arm and peered out the window.

Within an hour, the body of Augusta Clarice was indoors, wrapped in blankets by the fire. By the time they reached her, the body was cold and lifeless. Thrush had waded through the deep, drifting snow and lifted his daughter gently, cradling her body in his arms as he made his way into the formal salon where her mother and sisters sat huddled together sobbing.

Elwood Addington Thrush could not bear it. He had dared to entertain the secret in his heart that Augusta Clarice was his favorite. In sharp contrast to the irreproachable equanimity and charm of the other three Thrush young ladies, Augusta Clarice was bold and defiant. She was an explorer of attics and river fronts. She was a teller of incredible, and incredibly preposterous and entertaining, lies. She was a hider from Mathilde-Eloise and a consummate avoider of tasks, the sort of tasks that build character in a young woman and ensure she is never vain or withdrawn.

The prankish girl had been a recalcitrant thorn in her mother's ordered and peaceful daily routine, and she had made everyone laugh in a household that was, by its very nature and careful design, reserved and distant from the baser sentiments that constrain the lives of lesser citizens among the rank and file. Augusta Clarice, from the earliest age, had been a dresser-up in ridiculous get-ups culled from the attic and a putter-on of shows, demonstrations, antics, and wild displays of unpredictable and youthful chicanery. And this, Thrush had known in a heartbeat, was what had drawn his daughter out onto the precarious ledge outside the open window of the observatory on the night of the first blizzard of the year.

In short, Augusta Clarice was absolutely everything that Thrush himself, as well as the more obedient and compliant members of his familial entourage, was not and could never be. And he had secretly loved her for this as he loved no other person in his life. And she had never known.

Mathilde-Eloise dried the body and dressed her in clean clothes and then brushed her long hair at Thrush's instruction. She had sent the girls to their rooms and tried without success to urge their mother to take some warm milk. The dinner sat cold in the kitchen. Fredreich paced with worry. Thrush attempted several times to elicit some small reply from his wife, who lay half draped on the divan, either willfully ignoring her husband or unable to respond to his entreaties.

After some hours of this, Felicity composed herself and rose stiffly then dried her eyes. She announced calmly that she was going to bed and issued a muffled, cool "good night" to her husband. Thrush turned to follow her but then considered her closed and silent demeanor and decided to remain behind. It had always been their custom to maintain separate sleeping quarters at opposite ends of the house with the children amply situated between them.

After dismissing Fredreich and Mathilde-Eloise for the evening and accepting their distraught condolences and tears, Thrush retired to his manly quarters with a snifter and a bottle of cognac, a libation whose company he rarely sought but which always seemed to induce a reliably deep slumber after only a glass or two.

He was awakened to the sound of a great commotion below and numerous voices in various states of distress and command. He leapt from his bed at the sound of unknown male voices and looked out the window. There were unfamiliar vehicles, three late-model sedans and a small, unmarked van, in the driveway. He could see Fredreich was out in front of the house, clearly directing traffic as numerous persons, complete strangers, shuttled back and forth between the waiting vehicles and the front door that lay wide open, casting the full light of the foyer and entry hall on the blanket of snow and the chaotic network of footprints that ruptured and dirtied its pristine surface.

Thrush quickly donned his dressing gown and slippers and hurried downstairs, exercising just enough decorum and control of his person as was required in the presence of strangers and unknown goings-on in his home in the middle of the night, the nature of which clearly involved both the complicity of his wife and children—and his complete ignorance—for their successful completion. Barreling down the stairs, his indignity and rage fully alight, Thrush came to a halt before the open towering double doors of the formal salon, clearly the seat of command for the current campaign of affairs.

It was then that he peered into the center of the great salon and beheld it. An image so startling and momentous in its scope and import that it would embed itself indelibly upon his psyche and inscribe the very fabric of the remainder of his days with its memory: the great mound of stuff, piles of luggage and mountains of clothes, boxes and bags all thrown on the pile, books and trinkets as well as a thousand small mementos of a life, of their life together, his wife's, his children's, and his own.

Within an hour, all was cleared away, carted off, and shoved into the waiting vehicles, and then along with his wife and his daughters, both living and deceased, all disappeared into the night, and he never saw the four of them ever again. Until one morning very many years later...

III

Over those ensuing years, countless and regular missives, letters, parcels, and cards were issued forth from the Thrush residence at the typical and to be expected intervals addressed to one or another or all of the self-exiled members of the family. These were directed to all the corners of the earth where the lonely patriarch believed his family might have found refuge and established a new outpost of the Thrush lineage.

Never was there the least response or reply, nor any hint that his fevered communiqués, entreaties, pleas, inquiries, and well-wishing were ever received. Even during the early years of Thrush's abandonment when he issued numerous and frequent cries for help out upon the ethers when curious and troubling developments threatened his well-being, his peace of mind, never was there the least flutter of interest or concern returned to the ancestral manse.

All had eventually, with time, as is inevitable in most human affairs, settled down within the walls of Thrushdom and came to resemble something of an ordered routine. The house was impeccably maintained according to seasonal demands. Temperatures inside the house remained crisp to bracing, but heat was not withheld when needed for the maintenance of good health and a modicum of basic comfort.

Fredreich and Mathilde-Eloise were never truly forgiven for their complicity in Felicity's abandonment of Thrush and her absconding with his surviving children on the night of Augusta Clarice's death. But they were peerless as household staff, and they knew the house and its numerous idiosyncrasies to precision and attended to them without complaint. As well they knew Elwood Addington Thrush to a degree that the lord of the house found them comfortable and would not have wished to suffer himself and the house the trouble and expense, and the uncertainty, of seeking out, hiring, and training new staff that in all likelihood would not be suitable at all to his tastes and various unique requirements of the house. So all remained as it remained for nearly forty years.

IV

nd then, on the occasion of her mother's death, and several years after the tragic loss of her two remaining sisters, Violette Marie Constance reached out to the only person yet to be informed of the sad news of the recent passing of her mother: her father.

Thrush found it exceedingly good fortune that his daughter had called, that she was indeed *in town* looking after various matters pertaining to her mother's considerable estates, and that she seemed completely amenable to a liveried drive up the river to her childhood home and a tentative reunion with her elderly father.

Fredreich and Mathilde-Eloise were possessed of an enthusiastic hopefulness that had not graced the walls of the house for almost four decades. They smiled to each other as they closed the doors of the formal salon after serving their employer and his daughter and accepting the woman's warm greetings and a brief word or two of shared memories. Then they retired to the kitchen to undo the work of the morning's preparations and put all aright once more in its proper order.

It was something of a shock then, when a mere half hour later, the doors to the salon burst open and the sound or angry heels on the marble floor destroyed the soft silence of the house. These were joined by raised voices and, while, of course, they did not open the doors and peer out at their employer and his daughter, they made no attempt to hide themselves from what rose enough to become sensible to their ears.

"I'm sorry, father," Violette Marie said, almost in tears. "I should not have come. Mother warned me, oh, how she warned me all those years while we were growing up," she continued.

"Violette, my dear, please, come back to the table and finish your breakfast, please," the old man cried out plaintively. "What can I say? You must believe me," he pleaded.

"Believe you? Father, I don't even know how to help you. You, you are truly mad!"

"No! Violette, no, I am not mad. Please, didn't you see, at the table while we ate? Give me a chance to explain! Surely you saw—"

"No! Stop it! Father, I read all your letters. All those years, mother had never let any of us see them. But she kept them, saved them, I'm not sure why."

Thrush's face brightened at this for the first time since his daughter's arrival.

"You read them?"

"Yes, when I was going through her things, I found them in a box. All organized by date and by year and by the recipient's name. Yes, she kept them."

"Well, then, you know, please," he began, but she cut him off.

"No, Father, no. I will not be a party to such madness, such, such," she faltered, her lips curling in disgust. "Father, you are not well, and I implore you to seek help. But this obsession, this…I cannot be a party to it. I'm," she sobbed. "I'm so sorry, I should never have come!" she cried and then fumbled around for her things.

Mathilde-Eloise heard all this and scurried from the kitchen to retrieve Violette's cape and hat and her bag. She handed the woman her things and then retreated to the kitchen where she left the door ajar just an inch.

Without even putting her cape on, Violette Marie grabbed her hat and bag and hurried out the door and up the walkway where she was helped into the waiting car by her driver, and then they were gone. Thrush was left standing in the doorway watching as the car disappeared, trembling and wiping his brow with his hand before turning and going inside and closing the door.

V

Elwood Addington Thrush sought neither the aid nor counsel of his servants but retired straightaway to the salon to contemplate the unfortunate and disappointing visit of his daughter and how he could have ever been so foolish as to hope that, after so long a time, there was any reason to hope at all. He noted that the dishes had all been cleared away and the table swept of crumbs and now, there was no longer the slightest evidence that Violette had even been there, besides the pain and disappointment that filled the old man's heart.

He sat down at the table and absently regarded the playing cards carefully arranged at his usual place on the table. His eyes narrowed as he picked up the cards and considered his hand as well as a variety of possible stratagems. His opponent was very shrewd and could be quite merciless at times and delighted at besting him at every turn. But he enjoyed certain other advantages.

"I told you she wouldn't believe you," Thrush's opponent said triumphantly as she eyed her own cards with a satisfied smile. "She was never very imaginative!"

Augusta Clarice sat before him exactly as she had looked on that Christmas Eve so many years before: the precocious twelve-year-old who had tumbled from the second floor observatory mezzanine into the snow and died there. But let it never be presumed that the dead do not progress in other ways besides their appearances.

"I had to try!" Thrush protested sharply. "They're all gone now, really...gone," he muttered sadly.

"No matter! I'm here, you're here, and we have Mattie and Fredreich to take care of us. He's such a dear, Fredreich is. He brought in my favorite blue roses for the breakfast. Wherever did he find them this time of year?" she said brightly. "Fredreich and Mattie believe in me," she continued. "They love me, and you of course, Father," she said with a smile as she pretended to stretch and peek over at his cards.

"Oh, my darling Augusta, perhaps I am truly mad after all," Thrush sighed.

"Why Father! Of course you are. Really and truly mad. Just as I am really and truly here. But you can be so silly at times. Whatever would you have done all these years without me and Mattie and Fredreich to take care of you?" she said, shaking her head. Then she got up and walked to the double doors, which opened silently before her.

"Fredreich, could you be a love and bring father another pot of coffee?" she called out.

"Very good, madame. And you, will the young miss be requiring anything special herself today?" Fredreich inquired from the kitchen.

"No, I am perfectly fine," she replied, resuming her place at the table. "I have everything I need right here in this house, Fredreich. Thank you," she called out as she picked up her cards and eyed them narrowly. "Go on, Father. I do believe it's your turn."

About the Author

Aaron Vlek is a storyteller and a graduate of Sarah Lawrence College where she spent most of her time writing. She also took numerous writing workshops at Sarah Lawrence Writing Institute. *Domine Canè*, a short piece of speculative horror with a historic theme, appeared in the current issue of *Bards and Sages Quarterly, Vol. VII, Issue II*. *The Black Meal*, a work of speculative horror appears in the October issue of *Outposts of Beyond*. *At the Kids' Table* appears in the Christmas Edition of *Chicken Soup for the Soul*. Additional stories have been accepted by publications in the U.S. and U.K. for 2016.

THE DARK WALK FORWARD

John S. McFarland

Lucie told her son he should call the bandaged man Daddy. She told him that this man, this stranger, was his father. The boy had little memory of him, and with the man's whole head wrapped in bandages, there was no face for him to recognize. The boy didn't seem to think it odd that he had no father at home since his mother took such good care of him. He never thought a father was needed. Lucie said this man had gone off to war and been terribly hurt. Burned. She had not spoken much to the child about the man because she never expected to see him alive again. She thought it best. The man survived the war, though his face had been burned away in a battle, burned so badly the doctors had taken skin from his legs and sewn it onto his face. He had gone through a long recovery in another country.

Now he was home. Daddy.

Though Lucie called the boy Trieste, he knew his real name was Charles, and that he was named after his father. He knew he was four years old but not like other children. He could not speak like them or play with them. Their noise and energy made him scream, and he could not tell them what was the matter when he screamed, so Lucie kept him away from other children. She moved him far into the country, away from the town of Ste. Odile. She told him she would teach him everything he needed to know herself. He tried to learn numbers and letters as his mother taught him, but he had a hard time remembering them and using them in the way she wanted him to. Especially numbers. He seemed to only be able to see them as things that were oddly alive and able to duplicate or reduce themselves endlessly, not as just marks on paper. He had always loved the old story of the salamander his mother told him, of how it was born from fire and crawled out of burning logs. When his mother wrote 3 + 2 on a paper, Trieste saw five individual salamanders wriggling out of a flame in his head, and he knew the answer to the problem was 5. Lucie slowly understood her son's way of seeing things, and she was patient and full of love for him. Even at four years old, Trieste knew this.

Their small house in the Saline Marsh was their own world apart. They had pullets and geese and a garden and a big, fighting terrier to keep the foxes away. Trieste named the big dog Rudy Benko, a name that popped into his head the moment he laid his eyes on it, that afternoon when their friend Marie gave him to them.

Their only neighbors lived a long walk north along Saline Creek: Genevieve Gothard, the wildcrafter, and her husband Mesmin. Genevieve had given herbs to Trieste's mother to cure her sadness and others which were meant to calm the boy and make him better able to be near other people and learn more easily. None of these remedies seemed to work. But after they had lived in the small house a while, Trieste seemed calmer, and he was learning a little better, and he noticed his mother became a bit more cheerful. Trieste's duties were to gather the eggs from the chickens every morning and to feed Rudy Benko. He enjoyed doing these things and felt that when he did them, he was adding to his mother's happiness.

Trieste made one friend in the few times he'd attended the Church of the Holy Mandilion in Ste. Odile. Her name was Ady Stauffenberg, and she was one month older that Trieste. Ady's mother, Marie, owned a car, and every few weeks, she and Ady would come out to visit them. Ady's calm and patient nature never upset Trieste or made him wish she were gone, and Marie and Lucie were great friends and always had many things to talk about.

Two months before his father was due home, Marie and Ady visited them. The mothers had coffee and toast with preserves in the kitchen while Trieste and Ady sat on the front room floor, cutting pictures from magazines and pasting them on paper to illustrate stories they invented. It was one of their favorite things to do. They had made four story books illustrated with pictures this way. They were only allowed to make their picture books where their mothers could watch them. Once they had gone into Trieste's room and set one of their books on fire. Trieste tried to explain to the mothers that he no longer liked that story book, and since he couldn't stand the idea that it would still be in his home after he no longer wanted it, he needed to burn it. Lucie told her son it was the only time she ever thought of spanking him.

"He has been in London for many months," Lucie said, refilling Marie's coffee cup. "He's had five surgeries to rebuild his face. He has been under the treatment of a Dr. Gilles. Harold Gilles, who has been treating soldiers with horrible injuries from the war: facial disfigurements, burns, shrapnel injuries, and the like. Charles' face was nearly burned away. Dr. Gilles is experimenting with a procedure where he replaces burned skin with skin taken from other parts of the victim's body. It's called reconstructive surgery, but they never look…the same. In fact, in spite of the surgery, the victims still look, quite grotesque, I'm told."

"Those poor men! Who would think a thing like that would work?" Marie said, sipping her coffee. "It almost sounds like the Frankenstein story in real life! Oh, Lucie…I hope that wasn't the wrong thing to say! I say such stupid things sometimes. Charles has written to you?"

"No. He is unable. He has lost sight in one eye and is nearly blind in the other. There is an orderly caring for him, Mr. Hogue, who has written me of Charles' progress. He says Charles is a shattered man, shattered…of course. Unpredictable and full of rage. Mr. Hogue hopes being home and that being with his family again will be restorative to Charles, give him peace, and make him the man he was before the war. But…how can that be? Marie, how can Charles ever be a father to Trieste again? How can he be a father to a child like that?"

The day Trieste's father returned to his family was a very hot August day. They could hear, above the sound of the cicadas, the car coming from some distance away, and so Trieste and his mother walked out into the yard to watch for their visitor. The car was a green sedan with US GOVERNMENT on the license plate. The car pulled off the road in front of their cottage and parked on the dry grass of their front yard. Trieste grabbed his mother's hand and held it tight.

"Is this Daddy?" he whispered to his mother.

"Yes, it's him," she said. "He has suffered very much. We must do what we can to understand him and make him feel welcome and… at home."

"But why does he have to come and live with *us*?"

There were two men in khaki military uniforms in the front seat of the sedan. The driver got out of the car and opened the rear door. The dark form of another man was visible in the back seat. The other soldier approached Trieste and his mother. He was carrying a red folder and a small leather bag. He touched his hat.

"Mrs. Barre? Lucie Barre? I'm Lieutenant March."

"How do you do, Lieutenant. I didn't expect…"

"I'm a liaison of the War Department with the office of the Supervising Surgeon General of the Public Health Service. As Dr. Gilles of the British Army performed experimental reconstructive surgeries on some American service men, the War Department and the Supervising Surgeon General have agreed to track the physical healing and psychological progress of these subjects and to keep Dr. Gilles and his associates informed so that their treatment of future wounded can be improved. Private Barre…your husband, was one of the more severe cases and is of great interest to Dr. Gilles and Dr. Trevellian, the alienist. They felt they were making no new progress with his mental state, his depression, and that keeping him confined in a hospital wouldn't be a real test of his ability to re-assimilate back into his old life. They thought he might do well to be back home with his family. This is all experimental."

"Experimental!" Lucie said. "But what are we…how are *we* to cure him? My son is special, unusual. He can't cope with this."

"He is your husband, ma'am. It will do him a world of good to be with you and your son again," March interrupted. He knelt down and looked Trieste in the eye. "You're Charles Junior, are you? You must be glad to have your daddy home?"

Trieste looked quickly at March and frowned. "I don't know who he is," he said and buried his face in his mother's apron. March stood.

"He needs your care and kindness, Mrs. Barre," he said. "He won't recover without them. Here is his file." He handed Lucie the red file and leather bag. "Remove his bandages tomorrow and do not reapply them. In the bag, you'll find morphine and instructions for its use. Also extract of aloe if he needs it. Keep him out of the sun and in a calm state. Don't cook if he is in the kitchen with you. He is terrified of fire, as you would expect. There is a journal in this folder. If you would keep a record of his progress, the Supervising Surgeon General will be in your debt. We need to gather information about these men. It's all new country to us. I'll be back to check on him in a month and bring you fresh supplies. You don't have a telephone?"

"We're not rich, Lieutenant."

The dark figure in the back of the sedan stepped out into the sunlight with the driver's help. Charles had become alarmingly thin and stooped, but seemed taller than when Lucie had last seen him. His head was wrapped in bandages. The driver took his arm and helped him walk slowly toward the house. Trieste broke away from his mother and ran inside.

"He's nearly blind," March whispered. "He has some vision left in his right eye, especially of things directly in front of him." Lucie walked slowly toward her husband.

"Charles," she said, touching his arm, "I never thought we'd see you again."

"Neither did I, Lucie," Charles said. His voice was wet and vague and his words were barely understandable. Lucie held his arm for a moment. She was uncertain about or unwilling to express any further affection.

The driver handed Lucie a small suitcase.

"We are going to leave you now, Private Barre," March said. "I'll see you in a month. Remember, healing will be slow, and your family wants the best for you. Understand this is difficult for them, too." March and the driver returned to the car and in a moment were out of sight along the dusty road.

Charles made a wheezing sound and swallowed hard. Lucie held his elbow and guided him into the house. At the front porch step, he tripped, and she steadied him. "You know I'm as good as blind?" he snapped at her.

"I'm sorry, Charles. I didn't think."

"I'm sorry. That wasn't much of a greeting, was it? Why did you move out here anyway? So far out here away from town?"

"It was best for Trieste. Charles junior."

"The boy has to learn to adjust, like I do."

In the front room, Lucie led Charles to his old chair, and he collapsed into it. He exhaled loudly as he sat. Lucie sat opposite him on the sofa. Charles' mouth was not bandaged. His lips were swollen and pink, and his teeth looked elongated and discolored.

"Are you hungry?" Lucie said. "Can I get you something to eat?" She stood.

"Just some water. Where's my son? I can't say how much I have missed the both of you."

"He's here. He may need a little time to get used to having you…"

"Where is he?"

Lucie could see Trieste's shadow from where she stood, behind her bedroom door. "Trieste, honey," she said, "Come here. Daddy wants to see you. He missed you."

"His name is Charles. Don't you want to call him by my name?"

"It's his nickname. It's what he's used to. Let's not argue about this now. Let's get him used to having you…to being a family again." Lucie walked quickly across the front room toward her bedroom door. She held her hand out toward Trieste, and after a moment he took it. "Come on, Son," she said.

Lucie led him into the front room. Trieste pressed firmly against his mother, refusing to look at the strange, bandaged man.

After a moment, Charles spoke.

"You don't remember me, but I'm your father." The words were garbled and indistinct. "Can you look at me?"

Trieste whispered to his mother, "I can't understand what he's saying."

She knelt down beside him. "He said he's your father."

"I *know* he is!"

"You'll be able to understand him better as time goes on," Lucie said. "You have to get used to each other again. It will take time, as Lieutenant March told us."

"I know you don't know what to make of me, especially looking like this," Charles said. "I won't force it. We have time. All the time we need. Right now all I want to do is rest. Lucie, I want to lie down for a while."

Lucie watched him walk into her bedroom, kick his shoes off, and collapse onto her bed. He had chosen the right side, her side to sleep. She went into the kitchen and heated up some succotash for Trieste.

The next morning, Lucie cut the bandages off.

Charles had had a restless night, and Lucie didn't sleep at all. Their double bed seemed suddenly small to Lucie, and she didn't see how she could ever get accustomed to sleeping with him again. When he touched her shoulder, she flinched and moved a few inches away from him. A few times, she felt herself drifting off to sleep, but at those moments, he would gasp for breath or say something about their wedding day or Trieste's birth at Bonne Terre Hospital and how they loved their new son, loved him even more as they realized the infant didn't respond to them and connect to them as a normal baby should.

In the morning, Charles said he was anxious to get the bandages off, and he insisted that Lucie do it before breakfast. Charles sat at the kitchen table while Lucie rummaged through the kitchen drawers looking for her scissors.

"Trieste," she said, "where are my scissors? You and Ady were using them…"

Trieste walked silently into the kitchen holding the scissors in his left hand. He was sucking his thumb.

"Oh, Son," Lucie said, "don't tell me you're sucking your thumb again. You stopped that months ago!"

"Get your thumb out of your mouth!" Charles said. "Are you a baby?"

Trieste ran into the front room and hid behind the sofa.

Lucie carefully placed the scissors blade under the bottom edge of the bandage and began to cut. As she cut, an odor of suppuration escaped from underneath. She turned her head away, choking, and thought she might vomit.

"On with it! Finish it!" Charles demanded.

Lucie slowly continued cutting, holding her breath for long stretches at a time. The interior surface of the bandages was wet and stained pink, and she shuddered when her fingers brushed against it. In a few minutes, she had cut the saturated cloth completely away.

"Oh, Charles!" she exclaimed, before she knew she had said it.

It was not a face but a mask of misplaced thigh skin which looked now like a crust of dry mud spread across missing features with holes for eyes crudely and unevenly punched through. It looked nothing like the face of a natural man but like a hideous impersonator in a disguise haphazardly put together. The eye-holes were mismatched: the right one small and round and the left one distended and oblong, incompletely covering the damaged flesh under it. The left eye was obviously sightless: a gray film covered it. The right eye fluttered and blinked painfully. The lips were swollen and red and stretched out from the elongated teeth which were always visible. The nostrils extended above their normal limit, well above the tip of the nose. There was a patch of hair left at the top of the head. Lucie gasped, and she heard her son in the front room crying. Rudy Benko was barking excitedly at something in the yard.

"Are you in pain?" Lucie asked after a moment. "Do you need the aloe?"

"I am always in pain. Look at me. How could I be anything else? Get a soft cloth and dry off the seeping areas. And shut that dog up. What the hell is he barking at?"

Lucie did as he asked. She dabbed carefully at the pink eye orbits, lips, and ears. "Trieste, see if you can quiet the dog down," she said. Trieste went outside.

Charles whimpered almost inaudibly. He picked up a hand mirror he had brought from his wife's dresser and looked. "Oh," he said. The word trailed off into a sob.

He stood and walked into the front room, drawing shuddering breaths as he tried to mask his emotions. Trieste came back inside and moved behind the couch. The dog had stopped barking. Charles sat in his chair and slouched against the back.

Lucie saw that the wet skin of his neck was touching the fabric. She thought to ask him to let her put a towel behind him, but she kept silent.

Rudy Benko started to bark again. Trieste ran outside and came back in immediately.

"It's a possum in the tree," he said. "Rudy Benko always barks at possums. I can't make him stop."

"Son," Charles said. His voice was weak. "Charles, come here. Charlie…Trieste. Come here a minute."

Lucie walked into the room. She stood at the back of the couch and held her hand out. Slowly, Trieste took it. He stood.

"Son," Charles said. "You need to look at me. Look and get used to it. The doctors can do no more for me. This is as good as I am ever going to look. We'll all be together from now on, so you need to get used to me. I know we can do it."

"But momma and me moved here," Trieste said, clinging to his mother's side. "You weren't here when we…"

"Where my family is, is my home. I am here, and I want you to get used to it. I am the only father you're ever going to have. Okay?"

Trieste nodded his head.

"I've been home since yesterday, and I haven't had a hug from my son yet. Now, I don't expect you to, not right away, but you could shake my hand." Charles extended his right hand.

"Give him more time, Charles," Lucie said. "This is so much for him to adjust to."

Charles exhaled painfully, dropped his arm, and seemed suddenly angry. "It's an adjustment for me, too! This is my family and my house. I am here to stay, so everyone better adjust! Look at me, Son. LOOK!"

Trieste looked timidly at his father.

"Get used to me and my face, boy. Get used to it, because I am here for good."

"I *know!*" Trieste mumbled. "You said it before. You keep saying it."

The next morning when Trieste got out of bed, he found his parents were up already, his father sitting in the front room having coffee. Lucie arose with her husband and made the coffee, serving it to him on the sofa. He sipped the hot liquid loudly, dribbling much of it on his chest from a mouth that never seemed to close completely. She returned to the kitchen to make breakfast. Trieste did not like the sound his father was making, and he went back into his room and put his fingers in his ears.

After breakfast and after Lucie had cleared things away, she prepared for Trieste's lessons for the day. In a kitchen drawer, she kept a book of the alphabet, a book of arithmetic, geography, reading, and penmanship. She stacked these on the table next to an Old Tecumseh tablet and a wide carpenter's pencil, newly-sharpened with a paring knife. Charles watched her as he refilled his coffee cup and returned to the front room.

"Why are you teaching him this stuff now? He's only four," he said.

"He's very bright," Lucie said, "but he has his problems, and I want him to have every advantage. He'll need every advantage. No time like the present."

"If you treat him like a freak, he'll always be a freak," Charles said as he shifted painfully on the sofa.

"He's not a freak!" Lucie said, looking angrily at her husband. "Don't call him that! Don't say that so he can hear it!"

"He needs to be in school with other kids. When the time comes, I want him in public school. If he doesn't learn how to be normal, he'll never be normal. It's just stubbornness in him, as I see it. What will the future be like for him if you coddle him like this?"

The phrase stuck in Trieste's head: "What will the future be like?"

"Charles, you don't..." Lucie stopped herself. She needed to be calm for Trieste's lessons. If she wasn't, he couldn't concentrate, and he would learn nothing that day.

"Don't think you can put me off, Lucie," Charles went on. "Don't think you can drop the subject or change the subject and then do what you want because I forgot about it. It's not just the two of you and me in the background keeping out of your business…I love him too, in case you've forgotten. We both decide what's best for him, not just you…" Charles' voice faded away. This burst of emotion had exhausted him.

A week after Charles' return, Trieste found he could stand to be in the same room with him. If his father spoke a few words, Trieste could tolerate it, but if Charles spoke more than a few sentences or tried to reprimand him or his mother, he ran from the room, disappearing under a bed or up a tree in the yard. This would enrage his father at first, but he didn't seem to have the energy to sustain his anger.

In the second week after Charles' return, they had visitors. Bill Wiek, wounded at Argonne, had lost his right eye, part of his jaw, and his right arm below the elbow. He had spent most of a year in a bed next to Charles' in the hospital in London. Both men found they had developed a taste for brandy while in France, and Wiek had promised Charles that if they both recovered, he would present his friend with a case to celebrate the fact. As good as his word, Wiek had just been mustered out at Fort Dix and was being driven by his younger brother Les, back to his home in Galveston.

Lucie offered the Wiek brothers dinner, but they declined, saying they would eat back in Ste. Odile where they had a room in which to spend the night before they continued their trip in the morning. Trieste stayed in his room, and after an hour of attempting to be polite and cordial as the men finished a bottle of brandy and started another, Lucie left them and sat with her son on his bed, reading to him until they both fell asleep.

In the morning, Lucie found the front door standing open, and Charles asleep on the sofa, drooling from his twisted, red mouth and snoring loudly. He smelled of alcohol. She decided to leave him there, undisturbed, for as long as he needed to sleep.

Just after ten o'clock, Charles woke, walked out onto the front porch, and vomited violently onto the Rose of Sharon bush. Then he went back into his room, got into his bed, and fell asleep again.

At noon, Trieste took his alphabet book, a pencil, and tablet out to the front porch. He lay on his stomach on the well-swept boards to practice writing his letters. A small squealing sound on the north side of the house was followed by barking as a possum ran past the porch and up the maple tree in the front yard. Rudy Benko was right behind the possum, barking wildly, nearly catching the animal before it skittered out of his reach. The dog stretched up the tree trunk as far as he could reach and continued barking excitedly.

"Rudy Benko, shut up!" Trieste yelled. "You're being too noisy!" The dog continued to bark nonstop for many minutes.

Suddenly the front screen door flew open, and looking back over his shoulder, Trieste saw his father standing behind him holding a heavy revolver that he had seen in his mother's chest of drawers once.

Charles had not noticed his son there, lying on the porch. Trieste saw in his head what would happen next but he could make no sound to stop it.

His father raised the gun and shot. Rudy Benko yelped and collapsed to the ground. Charles shot again, and red spray blew from the dog's head onto the tree trunk.

As Charles lowered the gun and turned back toward the house, he saw that Trieste was on the porch and had witnessed what he had done.

"Charles!" Lucie screamed as she rushed out the front screen door. "Are you out of your mind? Are you insane? How dare you!"

"Can see well enough to shoot a damn dog…if you thought I couldn't," he mumbled. "Damned dog that wouldn't shut up." He walked back into the house, feeling his son's eyes on him all the way.

Trieste made no sound. He put his thumb in his mouth.

Lucie looked at her son. He looked back at her, his expression as blank as when he had watched the first snowfall last winter. His mind had vanished into some other place, as she had noticed in him more and more as he got older.

"Son, I am so sorry…"

Lucie took a spade from the shed behind the house and buried Rudy Benko under the tree where he died. Trieste tried to help her, but she sent him to the back yard until she finished the job.

Late in the afternoon, Lucie put a pot of water on the stovetop and began to cut up potatoes into it. Trieste sat at the small kitchen table drawing the troll under the bridge from the story of the Billy Goats Gruff his mother had read to him the night before. As Lucie set the table, she noticed Trieste's troll was nearly bald with a tuft of hair at the top of his head, and he had a single eye. As Lucie watched him, Trieste drew a circle around the eye.

"Momma," he said, never looking up from his drawing, "why does he have to live with us?"

"You should stop asking me that question, son. He will be here from now on because he belongs here. We all just have to get used to each other. I'm sorry about the dog and sorry you saw that happen. All I can say is, your father is not himself yet. He would have never done something like that before...You'd better put that away," she said, nodding toward his drawing. "We'll be eating soon."

Taking a match from a box on the shelf above the stove, Lucie struck it and lit it. The blue flames engulfed the bottom of the cooking pot. A terrified moan came from the kitchen doorway. As Lucie and Trieste turned, they saw Charles falling backward against the china cabinet in the dining room.

Lucie gasped.

"Oh, Charles, I'm so sorry!" she said.

Charles groaned in pain and struggled to get to his feet. "Lieutenant March told you about that! He told you not to light a fire near me!" he screamed.

"I didn't *see* you there, Charles! If I had known..."

Charles stood silently for a few moments. His breathing was erratic and he appeared shaken.

"I'm okay. I'm okay," he said. "Not your fault. I came to say I'm sorry about the dog. I wanted to say I'm sorry to both of you, especially you, Son. A terrible thing to do..."

Trieste said nothing and continued to draw. Trieste was learning that he could stop hearing the arguments his parents had or anything they said. He could make himself stop listening and think about other things and places no matter how close or loud his parents were. He sat at the table, his drawing in front of him, and he watched the blue flame roiling under the pot. He imagined he saw a salamander, newly-made and perfect, wriggling free of the flames.

In the evening, Charles said he was thirsty and needed a drink. He took a bottle of brandy from the pantry, opened it with some difficulty, and returned to his chair in the front room.

As Lucie cleaned up the kitchen after supper, headlight beams flashed across the wall. The front door was open, and she recognized Marie Stauffenberg's gray Ford. Ady pushed open the passenger door and jumped out of the car.

"Who is that?" Charles demanded.

"It's Marie Stauffenberg and Ady, her little girl. They are friends of ours. I can't imagine what they are doing here now." Lucie dried her hands and hurried out the front door. "I'll see what they want Charles. You can just stay here, I'm sure they won't stay…"

Trieste ran out the front door ahead of his mother and out into the yard. He hugged Ady, who seemed surprised by his excitement. Lucie followed close behind him.

"Marie, what a surprise," she said.

"I'm so sorry to drop in on you like this," Marie said, " We haven't seen you in a while, and we had to go by Ady's grandma's to get her prescription filled, and I wanted to return your juicer. I found mine under the sink! And I wanted to see how things are going with Charles back…"

"Oh, Marie," Lucie said in almost a whisper. "This isn't a good time. He has been drinking. He has taken up drinking…"

With a terrified whimper, Ady suddenly ran to her mother and hid behind her.

"Child, you like to knocked me over…" Marie began.

"Why are they here, Lucie?" Charles had appeared on the porch. His speech was noticeably slurred now. "Don't you want them to come in?"

"Momma!" Ady was in tears.

"Be still, honey," Marie whispered. "I'm sorry, Charles. I never just drop by. I'm Marie Stauffenberg. Rude of me. We're going. We're going now."

"Go on then. If you're sure you don't want to sit and talk…have a face to face…" Charles mumbled.

Marie looked at Lucie for a long moment but said nothing more. Marie helped her terrified daughter back into the car. In a moment, they were gone.

Charles went back into the house and returned to his chair. He took another long drink of the brandy, spilling much of it on his shirt.

Lucie and Trieste remained in the dark yard for many minutes. Lucie knelt down next to her son.

"Ady was frightened," she said. "She wasn't expecting to see your father like that. We didn't have the time to warn her, did we? People who don't understand what your daddy has been through, won't understand…"

"I know, Momma," Trieste nodded. "People will always be scared of him because he looks like that. Grown-ups and kids. Always. And we will always have to live with him." He took his mother's hand. "Come in with me." He led his mother up to the porch and into the front room.

To Lucie's surprise, Trieste led her to Charles. The two of them stood in front of Charles for a few moments.

"Well?" Charles said, at last.

Trieste looked directly into his father's dead eyes, which he had never done before that moment.

"I want to know why you want to live in a place where nobody loves you?"

"Trieste!" Lucie gasped, as she pushed the boy behind her.

Charles stood in a rage. He reached drunkenly for his son, but Lucie pushed him away, and he fell back onto his chair.

"Go to your room, Trieste!" Lucie cried. "And lock the door!"

Trieste did as his mother told him.

Trieste heard a crash as though a chair had been thrown over. "You turned him against me!" his father screamed. "You haven't done anything to make this work!"

"I won't argue where he can hear us." Lucie said. "Come outside."

The back screen door opened, and Trieste could hear their voices out in the dark yard, fading slowly as they moved toward the woods. He looked out his window but could see nothing beyond the small oval of light from the open kitchen door on the black grass. Their voices were further away now, but he could still make them out as they moved toward the salt marsh.

"You hate me. You wish I had died over there…"

"That's nonsense, Charles! You can only see your own pain. You haven't tried to understand what *we* are going through. What about *us*?"

Trieste heard his mother make a sound like she had made once when she tripped on a root and fell. A little moan of muffled pain. Then he heard nothing at all for a very long time.

The darkness was silent, and suddenly Trieste felt there must be silence across the whole world. Everything was quiet and muffled, and he knew was alone. Knew he was the only living thing in the dark world, a ruined world, and that things as alone as he was could never find happiness.

After many minutes, Trieste heard the back screen door open. He heard footsteps outside his bedroom.

"Go to bed, boy," his father said.

"Where's Momma?" Trieste said. "She reads to me."

"Not tonight. She's upset. She's walking to…cool off. Go to BED!"

Trieste sat on the floor under his window. He knew his life was now broken and could never be repaired. He knew he was alone or worse: he knew he could do nothing but share his life in this small, isolated house with this hideous man. Trieste knew this was impossible.

Trieste did not move from the floor for more than an hour. He didn't expect to hear his mother come home again, and she didn't. He could hear his father snoring in the front room, and he knew he would be snoring still in the morning and that his mother would not be there with him. He opened his door and went into the kitchen. He pushed a kitchen chair next to the stove and found the box of matches on the shelf above it.

As soon as he entered the front room, he could smell alcohol. It was a smell that was familiar to him now, and which he never wanted to smell again. His father had spilled much of it on himself as he got drunker, before he fell asleep.

Trieste approached the grotesque man snoring in his chair. For a moment, he watched him struggle to draw air through his swollen lips. Fire could never make something as perfect as a new salamander, he knew: it could only make a monster like this man.

Trieste struck a match, and when he dropped it on his fathers' chest, he was surprised at how the flame leapt up as though it were anxious to be born.

The man, Charles, who called himself father, awoke suddenly and screamed. He swatted frantically at the flames, screaming and crying in pain and terror. His panic spread the flames across his alcohol-soaked body, and he fell to the floor, setting the sofa alight, screaming as he was consumed.

Trieste ran into his room and crawled under his bed. He knew the flames would never reach him. He knew it because there was no such image in his mind showing that he would be hurt.

In a little while, the fire had died down and there were cars in front of the house. A man out on the highway had seen the smoke above the trees and had come to help. He had sent another driver to get the fire department and sheriff in town. The man was a farmer who had been to a tavern. He came in through the back door and found Trieste in his room still hiding under his bed.

In a short time, the Sheriff was there, and a fire truck, but since the fire was nearly out, they just watched the scene to make sure a fire didn't grow or spread. Soon after that, a large woman in a black car arrived. She told Trieste she was from the state and that she was there to look after him and take him to a safe place. The large woman was very kind and had a soft voice that made Trieste feel less alone. The woman gathered some of Trieste's clothes and a few wooden toys. She asked him if he was ready to go. The only answer he could make was, yes, he was. After all, he knew he could not live in a half-burned house alone. The thought would have frightened his mother, and he would feel very bad to frighten her. He moved toward the front door.

The large woman's hand was on his head, gently guiding him toward the waiting sedan. He stepped across the threshold out into the night. With her kind encouragement, he started the dark walk forward toward the car and to all the ruined years to come.

About the Author

John McFarland's work has also appeared in the anthologies *A Treasury of American Horror Stories*, (along with work by Stephen King and H.P. Lovecraft), *Solstice*, and *Reconstructing the Monster*. His work has also appeared in *National Lampoon*, *The Twilight Zone Magazine*, *River Styx*, *Xharon*, and *Tornado Alley*. Aside from *The Black Garden*, his young reader novel about Bigfoot, *Annette: A Big, Hairy Mom* was published in 2013 and the sequel will be out in May 2016.

EDEN

A. O'Neal

The world ended on October 1. Because mass communication is non-existent, there's no consensus regarding what precipitated the Infection. Campfire lore and the ramblings of the disgruntled and displaced suggested it was a new cancer drug that awoke something in the cells of the users, or it was the result of bioterrorism. Maybe it was truly black magic. Perhaps it was nature's way of fighting back. Either way, it happened.

The Infection's effects on the body are grotesque, the stuff of nightmares. Before civilization collapsed, CNN and Fox News fueled the panic with gore-porn, recycling images of the terrible symptoms of the Infection. They seemed fond of one particular image of a small child clutching his heart to his open chest, as though it was a bird trying to escape his grasp. His eyes were simultaneously glassy and alert, unable to register anyone around him but hyper aware that death was close by.

Before Hell broke open and unleashed its despair upon the Earth, a Pentagon doctor developed a device that supposedly identifies the illness, even detects it before the symptoms appear. Little wands, much like the wands used by airport security, that beep when it gets within three inches of an infected person, were passed out at hospitals in the Southeast. No one had time to test its accuracy, but so far I've never had a false negative. I found it comforting that somehow medicine and technology could identify the Infection. That had to mean it was something natural, not inherently evil. This wasn't some shaman's curse run amok, I reasoned. These devices made it all the way out to the middle states before everything shut down.

And everything went down fast. On Monday, CNN was running a story about an "Infected child" in Africa, and by Friday, the entire Western world was in a panic. After that, Tennessee didn't get news anymore.

On the Wednesday before the world ended, I'd returned home only to find my family dead. They'd been shot and our house cleaned out.

I set fire to the house. By acting out this crass cremation, I alone could hold onto the memory of the life I once had with the people I loved. No one else would ever know the life I lived there, nor could they infer anything about the people I loved. The memories could never be appropriated by someone drifting by their remains. They would be mine for the remainder of eternity.

I packed what I could and left for Johnson City with my boyfriend Brett, hoping that a city with a bigger population and one of the best hospitals in the eastern side of the state would be safer, or at least saner.

I was wrong.

Stores had been broken into and looted. Wrecked cars lined the streets. Only bones of those whom the Infected had consumed remained. Not even animals dared to venture out into the sunlight. Before we discovered the hospital, Brett and I came across a group of fraternity brothers in a mostly destroyed Waffle House. They stood over the body of a small boy.

"What happened?" I asked.

"He was hiding in the closet. I thought he was one of them," one of the brothers cried. He pulled a revolver from his hoodie and shot his brothers without a word. He looked at me with tearful eyes and said, "I'm sorry but I only got one more shot." I held Brett's face away from the carnage as the brother's blood splattered across the grease-smudged window of the building. I prayed for their souls, prayed that they could find peace now that they had escaped Armageddon.

I looted the bodies, obtaining some change and a small Zippo lighter. Brett asked me to leave the gun. I conceded.

They say that hell is materialized through war, but a pandemic is a more accurate description. There was no "good" or "bad" side, there were no morals fueling the violence. There wasn't even greed—everything was random, and Death showed no preferences or prejudices. It was order-less and chaotic, and we couldn't hide behind man-made causes and values.

Finally, after two days of aimless walking and cowering at every suspicious sight and sound, we found the Johnson City Medical Center. The West Wing and the South Tower were virtually destroyed in a fire. Brett, who had stayed up to date until the very last transmission, explained that this hospital had taken Infected victims, but it had been evacuated during a fire. It was estimated only a third made it out alive.

The hospital was a miracle really, a large building, equipped with beds, stocked kitchens, and medicine. Brett and I explored, combing through closets and stairwells and the rooms that were still accessible. Most of the building had crumbled, but the East Tower stood sturdy and proud, largely unaffected by the fire. The East Tower became our new home.

The fire had started in the neonatal center on the third floor, and quickly took out the upper levels, as well as the west side of the building. The parts that weren't directly affected by the fire were dilapidated. Only about a fifth of the hospital was intact. At least, intact enough to provide a decent shelter.

Brett had vomited at the sight of the burned bodies. I found great comfort in them. If it was a germ or bacteria, something science could explain, then it was likely killed in the fire along with the patients who resided here. We were probably safer here, because charred flesh meant no Infecteds. Fire was cleansing. We could start again here.

We found usable supplies on the upper floors we dared to explore. Pain killers, water bottles, various surgical blades. The freezer in the cafeteria had remained cool despite the power outage, thanks to the unusually cool fall and the doors remaining closed. And we found what we would later call The Wand, the tool that would decipher who lived and who died.

"We can stay here," I told Brett.

He didn't say anything. We barricaded the doors that night with random debris and slept in the lobby.

I held Brett when he woke up screaming. I kissed away his tears. This was the Eden that I created.

∴   ∴   ∴

A week later, we took in our first Survivors. A mechanic named Bubba and his five-year-old stepdaughter, Anna-Marie, climbed up the collapsed third floor and made their way down to the first level, where they found Brett and me.

"Can we stay here?" Bubba asked.

And my heart broke for him. We stood at the end of the world, and Bubba had asked for my help. He appeared to be in his mid-thirties, a lifetime of smoking and drinking doing little to keep him young, but he still asked to stay, paying no attention to my youth or physical strength. In that moment, this hospital became mine and with that question, he became mine to protect and provide for.

We scanned them with The Wand. Both were clean. I opened my arms and embraced them.

"You will have certain duties around here," I told him that night as he ate.

He nodded. Brett kept Anna-Marie in his arms, rocking her to sleep with the half-burnt teddy bear she'd discovered in the neonatal remains.

A few days passed before Bubba went to retrieve some knives and firearms from a pawnshop near the hospital. I told him he would have to be rescanned before he could rejoin us. He didn't argue. He kissed his daughter goodbye. I said a prayer for him.

He returned with a Red Flyer wagon full of tools and weaponry. I was relieved when the scan came up negative. He also brought with him five new faces. Two were ETSU bioscience graduate students, Anala and Ravi; one was a homeless Gulf War veteran who called himself Thor; and a twenty-year-old named Beth and her younger brother Ethan.

"Ethan," she told us, "hasn't spoken since they came for our parents."

Once again, we were lucky. Their scans were clear. We let them in.

After a day or two of finding beds and medicines and food for these newcomers, I developed a deep sense of purpose and loyalty to these people. They were mine. God sent them to the hospital so that I could care for them when there seemed to be no hope in the world. It was my duty to care for these people, to provide for them, to protect them. And I vowed that I would do right by these people. I would reinstate order.

This was the Eden that I created.

∴   ∴   ∴

Soon, more people started showing up at our door. We had to send away two-thirds of the people that asked for our help. Our first positive was exceptionally hard.

I was testing them at the front of the building. We'd barred all other entrances so no Infected could just wander in. That day, about ten people had showed up from North Carolina.

"We...we need help," said the leader of their company. She was a short, squat woman with a soft face. I thought she could be an elementary school teacher. "We've been traveling for days and...we just need some food and some water."

"I'll have to test you," I answered. Getting their hopes up when there was no guarantee seemed sadistic.

"Test us?"

"We're not giving our supplies to people who test positive for the virus or whatever it is. We're only giving to the healthy."

When I pulled out The Wand, the leader wrinkled her nose. "Aren't those wrong half the time?"

"No false negatives," Brett answered. Bubba had followed him outside, armed with a rifle just in case there was trouble. "Better safe than sorry."

The woman thought it over, her followers trying to persuade her to either move on or do as we asked.

Finally, she consented. "We'll do it."

And I scanned them. She revealed her name was Barbara Fuller, and she was travelling with her family, which included her husband and their two children, her mother and father and her sister and her boyfriend and her boyfriend's son. Fuller's daughter was six months pregnant. I initially sneered at her, being pregnant in her mid-teens, but then I was overwhelmed with sympathy. She looked frail and overworked, and she couldn't quite catch her breath. To make such a mistake right before the apocalypse must have been heartbreaking.

Barbara and her husband were negative. Her daughter Gail, sixteen, was negative and so was her fourteen-year-old son, Max. The Fullers were thrilled. In hindsight, it seemed obvious that they would be; not only would they receive food and water, they weren't sick. Walking around for weeks wondering if you'd been Infected must've been pure hell. Bob Fuller raised his hands and praised God. I smiled.

Next, I tested Barbara's mother Pauline and her father Jerome. Pauline passed. Jerome did not. He paled. He reached for his wife's hand but immediately stopped himself. His chapped lips parted as he tried to say something but nothing came out. Shaking, he covered his mouth and tears welled in his eyes.

"There must be—"

"Pauline," Jerome croaked, "get in there and—"

Pow

Jerome's eyes faded out of focus, and he hit the ground before the blood started flowing. We stared, dumbfounded. Finally, I whipped my head in Brett and Bubba's direction. "Guys! What the hell?!" I felt sick.

They stared back like deer in headlights.

"Max," Barbara whispered.

I looked to the boy. He was holding a small handgun, his own face pale and wet with tears. It fell out of his hand as he collapsed to the ground. Pauline wailed, "No, no, no, what have you done, you wretched boy! Oh, you little bastard, how could you do that to your grandfather?" She came after him, wrapping her hands around his throat. "You ungrateful little bastard!" Tears rolled down her face.

Barbara and Bob wrenched their son free while his aunt Carla held her hysterical mother.

"I—I had to, Mom," Max whimpered. "He was gonna die of thirst or hunger or get eaten. This was..." he broke into sobs, "this was easier, Mom. Mama, I had to. Mama..." He broke into a mantra of "mama" while his father rocked him back and forth. His mother just stared at him as though she was seeing him for the first time.

I looked at Brett. He vomited. I wanted to as well, but these were my people now, and I couldn't be scared or upset when they already were. They needed peace for now, and I was offering that to them.

"Go inside," I said to Barbara softly. "I'll take you to your rooms in a moment, but let's get Gail here out of this sun." She nodded, her gaze empty. Bob and Max followed, but Pauline wept over her dead husband.

"Bubba," I said after I'd tested the remainder of the family (no more positives), "will you take Pauline out and let her pick a place to bury her husband?"

Bubba nodded. "Lemme getta shovel."

Bubba was a good man. Over the next two months, he repaired the generators that were damaged in the fire, rewiring them to work with solar panels. Soon we had hot showers and working stoves, meaning we could stop making fires in the trash cans to cook frozen hamburger. Brett started a large garden in the remains of the neonatal center and taught the rest of us to care for the growing vegetables.

This was the Eden that I created.

∵ ∵ ∵

Turning people away for positives got easier and easier. Many begged me to let them in. Others threatened me. But I stood firm in my resolve. "We can't waste supplies on the Infected. I have to take care of these people. I have to use my resources wisely."

Bubba took care of the ones that got violent.

The three months following the apocalypse brought me about five hundred people. I had no doubt that God had His hand in this. All these people, *five hundred* people found me in the midst of a catastrophe, and I provided them with everything they needed.

Gail's baby was born in our hospital. He was like our own. All of us saw Adam as proof that the human race would survive, that we collectively would make it through this horror story.

Adam died three days after he was born.

My people wept.

Barbara came to me one night while I was pulling my shift as lookout from the collapsed helicopter pad on top of the hospital, still the highest point amid the devastation. She skipped the formalities; we always did. When everything stopped, the need for niceties and politeness ended; we were open and honest, but we never stopped being good people. We may not have maintained society but we maintained our humanity, and I was proud of my people for that.

"I don't know how to go on, Sam," she said to me. "The sun keeps coming up, and I just want to tell him there's no point. It's over. The world has ended; your services are no longer needed. And yet...every morning, here he comes. And now my grandson…. The sadness was a thick, dull pain, you know? And I felt it everywhere, like my whole body had been thrown against a wall. But Adam...and my dad…." The tears poured down her face but she maintained her composure. "It's so sharp, you know? Like being stabbed. And I'm so mad!" She gritted her teeth, her words coming out in soft hisses. "The sun keeps fucking coming up, completely unaware that my grandson and my dad have fucking died! The whole world needs to stop because they died!" She wiped away the tears, sniffling. "But it doesn't. All my pain, all the pain of the people in this world, it doesn't mean a thing. The sun in the sky doesn't need us. He just comes up every day. Each day passes."

I took her hand, pulling her into my arms, rubbing her back. I said nothing; comfort seemed so meaningless nowadays. All I could do was embrace, and somehow that seemed to ease the pain. My people were hurting, and I was helpless to fix that, but somehow just holding them in their darkest times gave them that little bit of strength necessary to move forward into the next day. I was glad to be of service.

These were my people; I would get them through. I loved them as a mother loved her children. I would protect them in the face of danger, and I would comfort them in their times of need. God had given them to me, and I would not fail them.

Our gardens flourished. Color and life quickly returned to the faces of the Survivors. One day, Anna-Marie laughed. The laughter spread to Thor. It was the first sounds of happiness I'd heard since the end of the world.

This was this Eden that I created.

∴   ∴   ∴

One night we had a break in. I didn't recognize the kids, but they claimed we had turned them away. They were about fourteen and ten, haggard and thin, and my heart broke for them. I ordered Bubba to take them outside and do another scan. They both ran positive.

"Please," the oldest girl begged, "please, we won't stay. Just give us something to eat! Please! We're so hungry!"

I closed my eyes. "You're infected. You won't be in pain much longer," I told her gently.

"No! No, you can't do that! You have to give us food! You just have to! Please!"

"I can't waste my resources on someone I can't save." I kept my voice even. "Do not come here again, please."

I shut the door on her, as she wailed loudly and continued to beg. In the morning, she and her brother were dead, killed by shots to the head. I didn't ask; I didn't want to know. I didn't speak about it at breakfast.

I stopped praying.

Our hospital became more and more of a utopia. Five months after the world ended, Gail got pregnant again, this time by a boy named Eli. As the leader, I took her aside to tell her that we simply could not afford for everyone to have children, that this would need to be her last pregnancy. She wept but agreed. I held her for a long time.

I appointed Barbara the head of our kitchen, and she elected five people to work with her. Brett headed up our green team, aka the people who grew our fruits and vegetables and herbs. Bubba started a maintenance team, who kept the hospital clean as well as safe. Anything that needed boarding up, Bubba's team was on it. Lastly we had our medical team, which was led by a pediatrician and a nurse who joined our ranks. Everyone was important; everyone was equal. My people were happy, and, more importantly, they were safe.

Then one night, Thor started rambling on about Anala and Ravi, about how they were conspiring against him, how they were descendants of Judas Iscariot, born to destroy him. He removed all of his clothing and sat unprotected in the freezing early March rain.

"What do we do?" Brett asked.

I steeled myself. I would have to protect my people. "Tonight, I'll have Bubba take him out back. I can't waste resources on the mentally ill."

Brett's eyes deadened. He didn't argue.

Anna-Marie didn't laugh again.

A few nights later, Anala came to me. "How could you do that to him?"

I'd almost forgotten the ordeal. The winter's shorter days hadn't been kind to our generators, nor had the cold. I'd spent the last three days trying to balance the energy we had with the energy we needed. "I had to. We were out of his medicine. Weren't you tired of being called names? Weren't you tired of the accusations?" I asked gently.

She licked her lips. "He was crazy. That was all."

"He was racist. And it came out when he was off of his medication. I have to protect my people. We can't afford discord from something as meaningless as skin color."

"It's just...sad."

I reached out to touch her shoulder. "It's also empowering. You're a Survivor, Anala. You survived the end of the world. You were strong enough, physically and mentally. Why should I take food and water from you to feed Thor? There's no guarantee he'll survive. I choose to protect you." I smiled gently at her. "You're safe. Take comfort in that." I handed her a fresh cucumber and kissed her cheek. "We're going to be okay."

I watched her leave, making her way to the room she shared with Gail.

At the highest point of the building, what we would later christen "The Crow's Nest," sat Bubba and Max, keeping watch. Bubba nodded in greeting when I joined them. Max never looked anyone in the eyes.

"Bubba," I said, "I can take over from here. We haven't seen any Infecteds in a few weeks." I patted his shoulder. "Go to sleep."

"I'm fine."

"You'll make yourself sick," I said fondly. Darkness pooled under his eyes, and his sun-chapped lips were white and peeling. "We need you, Bubba. Take care of yourself. I've got it from here."

Bubba shook his head, but complied. I listened to his footsteps echo through the halls until he climbed into bed. Only moments later, I picked out his soft snoring from the others' sounds of sleep.

"I wanted to talk to you, Max."

He paled.

"It's nothing bad." I wrapped my arm around his shoulders. "I wanted to make sure you are okay."

He shook his head and said nothing. As a young teenager, one of the things that I had learned from my therapist was that people usually wanted to fill up silence. In other words, sometimes the best way to get someone to speak was to remain silent and be patient.

I studied his face for a long time. He opened his mouth to speak but quickly closed it again. I rubbed his back. He did it again, and then again, and I waited patiently.

Finally, he said, "I killed my grandpa." A dam burst inside of him, and he was sobbing. I pulled him to my chest and rocked slowly.

"You had to, Max. He would have suffered otherwise. You did the right thing."

"He might have survived," Max managed. "He could've made it. He survived the Korean War, he could've survived this." He wailed loudly, and I brought his head to my shoulder to muffle the sound. "And I took that away from him."

"Max," I whispered, "you did what you had to do. You did the right thing. You protected your family. You made sure we all survived. We couldn't do this without them. We couldn't do this without you."

His tears faded into exhaustion and soon he was asleep in my lap. The next morning, life seemed to have crept back into his face. I smiled, knowing he was a Survivor. These were my people, my Survivors.

This was the Eden that I created.

∵   ∵   ∵

Six months after the world ended, our numbers reached close to eight-hundred. Bubba's and Brett's teams worked together to restructure the rubble into a new makeshift tower around The Crow's Nest. It stood four stories above the ground and provided security teams a new vantage point, protecting us from raiders and the Infected.

Ravi rebuilt a CB radio found in one of the ambulances. He approached me with a request to head up a scavenging team.

"Why?" I asked. So far, I'd denied all requests to leave the hospital since Bubba returned with weapons in early October.

"I want to up the wattage on the radio. We can't be the only place in the world that has survivors."

"Why would we want to find them?"

His eyes met mine. "What if they need us?"

What if they did? I would turn away no one in need, as long as I was actually capable of saving them.

Since Thor's death, I was unsure of where Anala's loyalties laid, and because of Ravi's close alliance with her, I didn't trust him to lead my people. I appointed Bubba to lead a party of fifteen, armed with guns and sedatives and the knowledge that they would have to be scanned before reentry. I held a brief meeting, asking my people what they needed, reminding them that all items must be scavengeable and available, and that there was no guarantee the items would be obtained. Among the requests were prescription eyeglasses, aloe for sunburn, fluoride, and binoculars, but mostly my people had everything they needed.

From The Crow's Nest, I watched them scatter about the ruined city as the sun rose in the cloudless orange sky. My stomach tightened whenever even one of them dropped out of my sight. I counted all of them obsessively, willing their quick return. I didn't leave The Nest until they returned at dusk, and I didn't rest until everyone tested negatively for the Infection. I embraced each of them.

"You are so important," I told them. "We couldn't do this without you."

In the coming weeks, Ravi and Eli worked on the radio amid a bout of food poisoning. Again, my people survived with minimal effects, thanks largely to our pediatrician, Dr. Dixon, quickly identifying the source and eradicating it from the kitchen.

In the seventh month, the Senator arrived. It was an unseasonably warm afternoon in early May, and his group of five-hundred showed up at the newly-erected electric gate, most of them suffering from the early stages of heatstroke. Even if they tested negative, I wasn't sure treating them was a wise use of my resources. Granted, we were well-stocked, but remembering the crushing anxiety I felt when I sent out the last scavenging team, I had no desire to organize another raid anytime soon. I went out to meet them, Bubba at my side with a gun and Dr. Dixon behind me with The Wand.

"Well, hello there," a man with a deep Southern accent said. He was dressed in a pin-striped slacks and a matching blazer, his dirty hair slicked back in an effort to style it, and the warmth in his voice didn't match the desperation in his eyes. "My name is Senator Robert Cuthridge." He offered his hand to Bubba, who didn't accept.

"Might be infected," Bubba grunted.

The Senator withdrew his hand, his smile never fading. "I understand, son. I completely understand. Now, we've been walking for months, and it appears y'all have plenty of space here, son. How can I get my constituents in here tonight?" He laughed lightly at "constituents."

For the first time since I accepted a Survivor, I felt emasculated. My authority had been questioned, and that would not stand. I nearly sent him away right then. My people needed a leader, and I would be the leader they needed, even if I had to fight for the position.

Bubba did not take kindly to the Senator's mistake either. Glaring, he jutted his jaw in my direction, aim fixed on the Senator's chest. "Ask her; it's her operation."

"These are my people. This is my hospital."

The Senator nodded, understanding dawning across his face. "Of course, of course, I apologize. I'm Senator—"

I interrupted him to control the ebb and flow of the discussion. "We don't take in the Infected, Robert. Everyone will be tested by Dr. Dixon before they are allowed entrance. Once they've tested negative, they'll have access to our supplies and shelter. Be advised," I told the group, "once you enter, you will be charged with certain assignments. We've remained safe and alive by cooperation and teamwork. I expect the same out of you."

"What happens if anyone tests positive?" the Senator asked. "Y'all know those wands aren't terribly accurate."

"These are my conditions, Robert," I answered, keeping my voice soft. "Please abide by them or please leave. These are my people, and I will do everything in my power to protect them. Surely you understand." I motioned to the vast crowd behind him.

"Of course, ma'am, of course."

From The Crow's Nest, Max and Eli kept watch, weapons at the ready. When an Infected reacted violently to a positive result, he was quickly and painlessly put down.

Two hundred and seventy-three people entered my hospital, and I provided them with medical care, food, water, and warm beds. During the night, three of them passed away, and I mourned their loss. They had reached paradise but could not reap the rewards. This was the first night that Brett did not share my bed. I worried that I'd lost his love. In the morning, I had Bob bury the bodies in plots chosen by their families.

The newcomers assimilated quickly. Two were screenwriters, and they began writing stories for a nightly program which followed dinner. My people had moved past simple survival and were now producing art. I glowed with pride.

This was the Eden that I created.

∵   ∵   ∵

With the influx of extra hands and a greater need for space came a new structure, and I termed the hospital Camp Phoenix because from the ashes of the fire rose a new, sturdy building which buzzed with life. This annexed building became living quarters, additional rooms and a library. Slowly, wildlife returned to the city, which was now overgrown with plant life. We settled into our new lives.

Ethan came to me one night while Brett and I kept watch from the Crow's Nest. "Miss?" he said. It was the first time I had heard him speak. His voice was small and broken from disuse.

I nearly wept with joy. "Yes, Ethan, what can I do for you?"

"There are, um, lots of deer, and I know you don't like people to leave, but...I think we could hunt them."

I smiled at him, so proud of the progress he'd just made in less than a minute. He spoke, and it was with a suggestion to help my people. "That's an excellent idea, Ethan. Can you hunt?"

He shook his head. "I could, um, learn though."

I wrapped my arm around his shoulder and pulled him close. "Good man, Ethan. That's the attitude I like to see." I gave him an affectionate squeeze. "Now, go to bed. I'll call a meeting in the morning, and you can tell the Survivors all about it."

Ethan reddened when his audience applauded his idea. "Who knows how to hunt?" I asked them. About twenty hands rose into the air.

A week later, we set up hunting teams of five. They would rotate on a monthly basis. The same rules still applied in terms of being scanned upon re-entry. About twenty others signed up to learn how to hunt so that they could contribute. Three experienced hunters would go out with two learners once a month. The next month, a new team of three hunters and two learners and so on.

My people were risking their security and possibly their lives for their communities. Again, I was overwhelmed with pride.

As I watched the hunters from the Crow's Nest, Ravi approached me, the radio in hand. "There are others," he told me in an awed voice. "In Virginia. They're holed up in a prison, and they need supplies."

Once more, I found myself grappling with reservations regarding sharing. Technically, these people had not come to me, and yet, Ravi had sought them out, and the relief on his face when he told me there were other Survivors gave me pause.

I had claimed the Survivors as my own, and the people north of us had survived. It was my duty to protect them. If there was a God, He had given them to me.

I called another meeting. "I wanted you to know," I told my people, "that Ravi has initiated contact with others."

Soon I was discussing trade with their spokeswoman Kendal. Eight months after the world ended, we were trading starter vegetables and feminine items for weaponry and chain-link metal to reinforce the areas around the electrified fence. But I never let my people outside of the fence. All of our trading happened through an opening in the gate.

We were safe and we were happy.

This was the Eden that I created.

∵   ∵   ∵

The trouble started ten months after the world ended.

One day at breakfast, the Senator took a seat across from me. I felt Bubba tense, but I patted his thigh to ease him. "What can I do for you, Robert?"

A plastic smile split his face. "Some of our tomatoes have blossom rot."

I nodded. "I am aware. Barbara told me. We still have plenty of tomatoes, and once Kendal's team ships in some new dirt, we will grow more."

He nodded his head. "Of course, of course. I shoulda known you were already taking care of that, sweetheart." He rose and turned to leave. Bubba let out a low sigh and picked up his fork to continue eating.

"However," said the Senator, turning on his heel, "if our resources are low, and I'm just spit-ballin' here, maybe we shouldn't be trading our healthy starter veggies for metal."

I offered him the kindest smile I could manage, given the rage that was coursing white hot through my veins. "Our resources are not low, Robert. We actually have a surplus of tomatoes and onions, but we do need more metal for the next stage in the wall build."

"Oh, I'm not suggesting that we eighty-six the wall build. No, I know how you feel about protecting our borders, and that's fine. A lotta people in here agree with you. No, what I'm sayin' is, instead of giving them our food, let's give 'em money."

Brett snorted, speaking up for the first time in two days. "They have no need for money, Senator." I flinched at the title spurting off of my lover's lips. "None of us do."

"Now, see, son, that is where you're wrong. When all this is over and done with, you better believe the United States government is gonna come out on top, and just like Miss Sam here, I want our people at the head of the class. We are gonna survive and thrive, just like she said," he flashed a greasy grin in my direction, "and the only way to do that when things go back to the way they were there is to make sure everyone's got money in their pocket."

"While I can appreciate your sentiment, Robert," I answered, "things aren't going back to the way they were."

"Samantha, dear, we can't live like this forever. America's all about progress. Do you really intend to have generation after generation live here in this little camp?"

My temper flared, and before I could stop myself, I was growling at him. "This camp is a good and safe place. It's simple, but it's helped nearly eleven-hundred people survive. Don't you dare insult what my people have created."

He nodded sympathetically. "I understand that, sweetheart, I really do. But you gotta have plans for progress, and it's gotta go beyond a bigger fence. Veggies are good, but lettuce," he chuckles here, "speaks much louder."

I narrowed my eyes. "Are you suggesting that we *buy* Kendal's loyalty? Because I doubt she'll fall for something so passé as cash."

"I'm not saying we *buy* her loyalty. I'm saying that we need to make sure that they do just as well as we do. We're just making sure that when the economy is restored, and we can go back to living like civilized folks, Kendal's people will be taken care of, too."

Brett shook his head. "Even if we wanted too, we don't have money. And most of the banks got looted after y'all declared a state of emergency."

"Excellent point, Brett. You're a smart kid. Maybe one day the two o' you can come work in my office," he chuckled. I didn't laugh. "I pulled two-hundred and fifty *thousand* out of one of my accounts before everything shut down. I'd be more than willing to share it with y'all if it means helping our people as well as those in Virginia."

"I appreciate your generosity, Robert, but there's no room for money for now. We need tangible supplies and so do they. That money is worthless."

He sat back in his chair, looking as though he had just uncovered some long-lost treasure. My blood ran cold, and I couldn't explain why. "I understand, I understand. You're right. You are so right, little lady. Thanks for your time. I really do appreciate how approachable you are, Sam."

He turned and left, his stride much quicker this time.

"I don't like him," Bubba hissed. "We gotta get rid of him."

"We can't do that, Bubba."

"Why not?" Brett asked. "That's what you did with Thor."

My jaw dropped. I looked him dead in the eyes. "Brett..." I couldn't find the words to accurately express my hurt.

"I'm sorry, Sam. That was out of line."

We ate our breakfast in silence. I tried to hide my anger and sorrow from my people. I watched them go about their day from the Crow's Nest, and I found great comfort in the smiles on their faces. I had done what was best for them, and their joy was proof of that. They gardened, they played, they ate, they laughed, and they talked. Some of the smaller kids took to drawing on the brick walls in the kitchen with burnt objects from the neonatal unit.

This was the Eden that I created.

∴   ∴   ∴

I nearly cried when Brett sat on the edge of my bed. I opened my arms to him. I would always take my people back, especially Brett.

He didn't draw nearer, only sat at the edge of the bed. "Sam, I'm worried."

I motioned him to me again, and again he didn't move. "Today at lunch, Eli paid Barbara twenty bucks for an extra pound of venison."

I laughed lightly. "She'll figure out it's not worth it soon enough, Brett. Don't worry about it."

"No, Sam, you don't understand. Eli didn't have any money when he first got here."

"So?"

"So, the Senator's been paying people to do things for him."

The anger started to swell up in my heart. "Like what?"

"Like his duties. Money is being passed around."

I shook my head, chuckling. "I don't understand. What are they going to buy? Everything they need is provided for them."

Brett was silent.

I nudged him with my foot.

"I don't know. Anala has been telling people that you've got a communist agenda. And she told some of the newcomers about Thor."

My eyes dropped to the floor. "I did what had to be done. He wasn't a well man. It was no secret what happened to him."

A tear rolled down Brett's cheek. "A few weeks ago," he started, "I...I gotta cough."

I nodded slowly, silently prodding him to continue.

"I can...I've been taking some cough medicine from Doc, but..." He licked his lips, picking at the callouses on his hands. "My dad died from lung cancer, Sam."

I grabbed his hand, smiling. "Brett, a cough doesn't mean you have lung cancer."

"I've been coughing up blood, Sam."

The news smacked against me like a rogue wave, leaving me breathless and stinging. For the first time since the world ended, I felt powerless, like I was lost out to sea, frantically searching for land or a ship but finding only water surrounding me. In less than a second, I was reminded of how infinitesimal the space that my body and my consciousness took up was, how very little control I had over my life and the lives of others. I had protected my people from the Infected, and I had protected my people from insanity, and yet, I was helpless to stop the abnormal cell growth inside the body of my lover.

And a moment later, I regained that control. "Coughing up blood doesn't mean lung cancer."

"There are genetic factors—"

"Your dad smoked, Brett. I'm sure it's fine. I'm sure it will pass."

Brett's face contorted as tears of fury poured from his eyes. "I could be dying, and yet you choose to waste your resources on me? You didn't afford Thor that courtesy!"

Another verbal stab, aimed directly for my heart. "Do you want me to kill you, Brett?"

"I don't want special treatment because I fucked you two months ago," he spat.

Had it been that long?

"I love you, Brett. You won't tell anyone but Doc about the coughing, do you understand? We need you. I need you. We couldn't do this without you."

"So the length of my life is measured in how long I can be useful? Tell me, when I can barely move anymore, will you kill me then?"

My jaw tightened. My fist physically ached to swipe across his cheek in one swift blow. I felt more than saw him retreat. His shoulders slumped, his eyes back on the floor, and in those three seconds that we sat in silence, I hated him. I hated him for being sick. I hated him for challenging me. I hated him for backing down. Coward.

"You may leave now, Brett."

The next morning, I called a meeting. The Senator and a few others chose not to attend. I had never mandated meetings, so I did not fault them, though I would make it clear that all meetings thereafter were mandatory.

"I've heard that money is being passed around," I explained. "While I understand your concerns and your motivations for accepting cash, I'm afraid I have to forbid it. Everything is equal and everyone has enough. I don't want shortages to come about because someone has purchased more meat, taking it from their neighbor's plate. There is no need for money. Furthermore, there isn't really room for money in Camp Phoenix—"

"We need money," Anala shot back, "because our value to the Camp only goes as far as our health does."

Heads turned to look at her. I could see the Senator smiling.

"I don't understand, Anala."

"When we get old, or sick, God forbid, what keeps you from taking us outside the fence and shooting us? Or rather, having Bubba do it?"

My eyes widened. I felt cold. "Anala, I'm not out to kill those who are sick."

"No, just those that are useless."

"That is not true."

"Then why did you kill Thor when he could no longer function without his medication?!"

"Because he was working against us. He was working against you! Think about what you and Ravi have accomplished since you arrived! Think about how far behind we would be if it weren't for the two of you."

"So then my worth only extends to what I contribute to the group?"

"No, Anala, of course not." My heart ached. "I care about you. I cared about Thor. I care about all of you."

"Then why don't you let us decide for ourselves what we can accept as currency?"

"While I understand the merits of accepting money, I don't want to create scarcity for food or water or space. We all need to work together to make sure that no one starves."

"That's not fair. I work my ass off studying under Doc and working with Barbara in the kitchen, but I get the same amount of food as a hunter who slacks off all day?"

Bubba got to his feet. "And what makes you think that the hunters slack off all day?"

"I know they get a day off of work to go out in the wilderness, which is off limits to everyone else."

I straightened my shirt and said in a calm voice, "Anala, I understand what you're saying. However, I watch from the Crow's Nest. No one is slacking off. What I admire most about the Survivors of Camp Phoenix is that no one takes advantage of the system in place. So far, we haven't had issues of stealing or wasting or shirking chores. I am afraid that with the introduction of money, our system will fall apart, and the Survivors won't survive. Money won't protect you from illness, but we won't kill those that are ill."

"Even if it's infectious?" Anala challenged.

I swallowed. "That hasn't happened Anala. We will cross that bridge when and if we come to it. I just want to protect you from the Infection and hunger. How can I do that when you want to steal food from your neighbor?"

"I don't want to steal food from my neighbor. I want a guarantee that I will still have food if my neighbor doesn't do his job."

A few shouts of agreement followed her sentiment.

"None of you! None of you will go hungry!" I shouted. "I will starve before any of the Survivors of Camp Phoenix do. Do you understand? There will be enough food. Hold each other accountable! This is not Big Brother; this is trusting each other. I trust that you will do the right thing. We've survived this long on trust. The bare bones of this building is trust. Do your job and assume that everyone else is. Trust that your brothers and sisters are doing the right thing. Trust each other, or we have no hope to survive!"

Brett shot himself in his left temple that night. Scrawled on the wall in burnt charcoal was "Trust each other to do the right thing."

I didn't cry. We buried him beside Adam in a quiet ceremony, which nearly everyone attended. Anna-Marie wept silently, her face stoic as she held her stepfather's hand. She placed the half-burnt teddy bear she'd clutched the night they arrived in Brett's arms and kissed his forehead before we tucked him into the Earth. I told him I loved him when everyone was gone.

I wish he could have heard me.

It quickly became known that Brett had killed himself because of his illness. It both weakened and strengthened my reign. Some believed that I had forced Brett to kill himself to reserve resources. After all, I did not feed those I couldn't save. Of those believers, some thought it was good thing—evidence of my dedication to the betterment of my people. The remainder of those believers, thought it was evil. I had no loyalty to those I claimed to love and that everyone would eventually have to face the threat of being "put down" if they got sick.

Others believed that I had no knowledge of Brett's illness, and that Brett had killed himself of his own accord. Within this sect, there were believers that I had brainwashed him. Others believed that he had taken my words to heart, that he was an example to us all. We live for one another, and we die for one another. He did the right thing, and so others must do the same.

Some had a renewed sense of purpose, a drive to survive and make the camp thrive. Others were distrustful, fearing that at any moment, they would be deemed "inefficient" and killed. The Senator and Anala fueled this flame. Still, Bubba and Max estimated that I had the loyalty of at least seventy percent of the population.

When had this become so political?

All I had wanted was a safe place for my people.

This was not the Eden that I created.

⠢   ⠢   ⠢

Twelve months after the world ended, the wall was finished. In case of an emergency, a switch could be pulled, effectively locking down the building, electrified chain-linked fence and sheet metal falling around the Camp, protecting my people and our resources from the Infected.

It became necessary to establish a task force to ensure that the rules were followed. While most of my people obeyed the rules about cash exchange, a few people continued to buy extra meat or vegetables. Eventually, Beth had to make an arrest. To quell any fear or riots, I had to address the Survivors.

"Eli has only been detained to stop old currency from being passed around. It's essentially stopping theft and fraud. He will be released in two days. This is not a punishment, this is our attempt to reason with him. We do not need an atmosphere of distrust but of cooperation. Eli has been a valued member of our Camp. We hope he will return to that old Eli who worked for his brothers and sisters, not against them."

"You want the money for yourself!" Bob shouted. Barbara glared at him.

I couldn't help but laugh. "Bob, my very dear Bob, I have no use for the money. At all. None of us do. We're trying to get rid of the money, not hoard it."

That night, Bubba discretely burnt the money recovered while I kept watch in the Crow's Nest. We hoped that with Eli's arrest, a message would be sent. We hoped that the Survivors would see that money would only complicate a perfect system.

I was wrong. Beth made two more arrests the following week. Ethan and Gail had gotten into a fight. Gail had, apparently, raised the price of tomatoes due to the root rot of the starters. Ethan had attacked her. Beth broke up the fight and brought them to my room. The Senator came to their defense.

"This *is* still the United States of America. These kids deserve a trial—"

I snapped back, "There is no trial. This is not the United States that you knew. The world ended, and we're starting over. You have tried from the beginning to upset what we worked so hard to create, but I'm putting a stop to it now, Cuthridge. If you want to stay here, you will fall in line. You will do your chores. You will contribute like a productive member of society, or you will leave. Do you understand?"

His eyes flashed dangerously. "So you insist on holding these kids without due process? No plans for a trial? You're just gonna lock 'em up like dogs?"

"Everything has changed, Cuthridge!" I shouted. My blood was boiling. "And no matter what you do, we're not reverting back to your broken system of law and order and economics. You can be a part of this camp like everyone else, or you can leave. It's up to you."

"So you'd let me outside?"

"With the complete understanding that you would never set foot within our gates again."

He started to speak but was silenced by Bubba stepping between the two of us. Bubba stared him down. The Senator's mouth snapped shut.

I turned to Gail. "What were you thinking? Why did you do this?" I asked. My heart was broken. "Why would you *sell* something when it's being given freely?"

Gail shook her head, one hand on her full belly. "I–I don't know, Sam. I just worried is all. I wanna make sure that I can take care of my baby when she comes."

I studied her for a long moment. "Why," I asked sadly, "do you think I won't take care of your baby? Have you spent a single night without food in your belly or a roof over your head?"

"No, but the Senator said—"

Bubba reached for the Senator's neck, expletives and insults on his lips.

"Bubba, let him go!" I ordered my head of security. I turned back to Gail. "Don't listen to him. He only wants to scare you. It's not true, Gail. Those pieces of paper he gave you have no value here or outside the wall. You don't need to put your trust in money. Put your trust in the Camp. I promise, I will take care of you."

Tears slipped out of her eyes. I brushed her hair from her face, tucking it behind her ear. I lifted her chin so that our eyes met. "Gail, I don't want to arrest you. You understand that I have to, right?" I fought back tears of my own as she nodded her head.

I sentenced Gail and Ethan to two days in a makeshift jail, during which time I had them write essays on what they loved about the camp, how the camp had improved when they joined. I just wanted their loyalty to the camp to be at the surface of their minds. I wanted their writing to reflect that this was heaven, and that they wanted for nothing.

They emerged from their cells with smiles on their faces. I hugged them. "Promise me this won't happen again." They did and were released back into the camp.

The week that followed was pure bliss. My people worked in harmony. I could see no division, no anger in their hearts. Even Anala seemed to have relented in her pursuit of my downfall. Gail gave birth to another little boy whose breathing and heartbeat sounded normal. She named him Daniel. My people adored that baby, lavishing him with blankets and toys and various baby food recipes.

The only spark of displeasure I could see was the Senator's. Bubba kept a close eye on him. My people faced no immediate threats as long as they stayed within these walls. As long as they were within my gaze, they needed nothing. Everything was as it should be.

I had no idea it was poised to end in fire.

∵   ∵   ∵

A group of a dozen showed up at the gate just as Barbara's team was serving breakfast. They were a haggard bunch, their skin hanging off their bones, their eyes heavy with exhaustion. It was the worst I had ever seen. I wondered if they were in the beginning stages of the Infection.

With Bubba at my side, I met them. "May I help you?"

"Let us in," a man in a dirty sports jersey croaked. "Please, let us in. We need water."

I studied the group, taking note of a young girl with what was likely Down's Syndrome. She had a sweet smile on her face, though it was somewhat tarnished by her thinness and fatigue. I wanted very badly to help her. To be completely honest, I wanted to keep her to show Anala that my reign was not ableist, that someone with a different mental capacity had just as much right to be in Camp Phoenix than anyone else. With the walkie-talkie that Ravi had refurbished, I radioed Doc.

"We have some new prospects," I told her, trying to maintain a gentle smile.

"Be there in a few," she answered.

"Prospects?" the man asked. He swayed, one of his companions catching and righting him. "Just...just let us in."

"Let me explain to you how Camp Phoenix works." I proceeded to tell him about my rules: no one gets in without being tested. Anyone who tests positive is sent away. Once inside, resources are not to be wasted on outsiders. Chores will be completed daily and under no circumstances was money to change hands. I asked them if they agreed.

One of the woman glowered at me. She asked me in broken English, "You send us away?"

"If The Wand says you are sick, yes."

"It's been a year!" she shouted back. "No more sickness."

"I have no way to confirm that. My people come first. These are my rules. You can abide by them or you can leave."

"When the last time you saw Infected, huh?"

Bubba gripped his rifle. "You can move on, ma'am. Ain't no one telling you you gotta stay here."

They stared each other down. I think the smell of deer bacon and sautéed peppers is what brought her around. Her shoulders sagged, and she said she would wait to be tested. The good doctor came out to the gate along with Barbara and Beth, the Senator and Anala close behind. I glared at the Senator and pointed him back inside. Had his fury become tangible, it likely would have killed me. His eyes burned with white hot rage, and I felt a small amount of satisfaction that I had stripped him of his influence enough that he could express himself more honestly.

"This is Dr. Gabrielle Dixon and her apprentice Anala Vora," I introduced them. "They will be scanning you for signs of the Infection today. If you are negative, Barbara and Beth will tell you a little more about the camp and help you get adjusted."

The first three were negative, and I was overjoyed to see the relief on their faces. I would meet with them later, to discuss their needs and what they could contribute to the camp. The fourth was positive. The fight in her eyes was clear as day when she said, "I don't have the Infection! No one does! It's gone!" Her voice wasn't pleading as most Infected were; it was furious.

"I'm not wasting my resources," I reiterated. "You may leave."

"Bitch, I'm not going anywhere!" she growled, lunging at me.

A shot sounded and she was dead before she hit the ground. I looked at the newcomers, their eyes wide as saucers as they watched their companion bleed out, a glower plastered on her face. I shattered the silence that followed with an order to continue the scans. A quick glance at Bubba assured me of his loyalty. His rifle was poised, an even, steady expression on his face. I smiled.

The girl with Down's Syndrome was named Katie, as Anala soon discovered. As Doc continued about her work, Anala came over to me to ask, "Well, do you think you'll let Katie in? I don't know how 'contributive' she will be." She did nothing to hide hatred of me in her voice.

"Of course, Anala," I answered, my level of sweetness matching her nastiness. "You mustn't be so closed minded. She's just as capable as anyone else here."

"Given your record, I didn't think you'd allow someone with a mental defect." Something about the way she said that made my blood run cold. Her icy gaze unnerved me. I realized then that she'd resigned her activities to discredit me, but there was no doubt she would stab me in the back at the first opportunity. I maintained my smile, hoping to ease her. "Anala, don't be ridiculous." I reached out to grasp her shoulder, but she abruptly pulled away. She was making it more and more difficult to love her.

Bubba came to my side, eyes fixed on Anala. "Everything all right?" The doctor's assistant walked away without answering. When she was working again, he leaned over to whisper to me, "I don't trust her, Sam. We gotta get ridda her. She's poison."

"Not now," I answered. I don't know if I meant we would discuss it later or if I meant we would kill her later. I didn't want to start down that path, didn't want to discover that much about myself.

Katie and her family were the next ones to be scanned. Ensuring that Anala's eyes were on me, I made my way over to them, ready to welcome them once they were tested. I smiled at the mother, who appeared too dazed to acknowledge me. Poor dears.

The father tested negative, then the mother. I reached out to shake their hands, noting their weak grips.

Katie, unfortunately, tested positive. I looked up and saw Anala's panicked eyes focused on me.

I ordered Doc to scan her again. It beeped once more. Her mother and father ran to her, clutching her close to them, and I could see the hysterics building beneath the surface.

"You have to let us in," the mother said in a hollow voice.

What was I supposed to do? Katie was Infected. Her parents weren't. No amount of maternal love could protect her from the Infection, and no amount of my love for my people could protect them from Katie. I swallowed thickly. I briefly considered having Bubba shoot her right then, to protect her from anything she would face outside the walls of the camp, and thus give her parents the freedom to stay with me.

I shook my head. "I can't let her in. I'm sorry."

The mother shrieked, startling Katie. "I'm hungry, mama," Katie whined, her voice shaking.

"Just—just give us some food. Please. Give us some food, and we will be on our way," the father pleaded.

"I don't waste resources on those I can't save." The cold voice coming out of my head seemed so foreign suddenly.

"You said," Katie cried, "you said we could have some food!"

I opened my mouth to speak, to apologize, to compromise—I don't know. I might have stepped forward to offer my condolences. I don't remember anything about that moment except everything seemed to move in nightmarish swirls of gray. I felt something dull split apart the skin on my arm. And suddenly there was red. Just a few drops beading on the underside of my forearm.

And then a gunshot and a series of distressed screams. I didn't look up, I just stared at the miniscule dots of blood on my arm.

"Are you all right?" Bubba asked me, bringing me out of my trance. I was inside the camp, leaning against the wall of the empty makeshift library.

I shook my head, a pathetic attempt to orient myself. "I'm fine. I'm fine. She didn't touch me."

Bubba sighed, relief washing over his face. "Thank God. I'm so sorry. I shoulda been faster."

I tried to laugh, but it came out as a forced cough. "You were fantastic, Bubba. As always. We couldn't do this without you." I took a deep breath. Bubba believed me. As long as he believed me, I was safe. He would protect me. "Are they still testing?"

Bubba nodded. "Don't worry. Beth came out when she heard the second gunshot. A few of 'em got kinda handsy, so only about five of 'em are left."

I wrinkled my brow. "Handsy?"

"Pissy that I killed the retard."

I winced at the term. "Watch your verbiage, Bubba."

He rolled his eyes. "And I thought the end of the world meant an end to all the PC crap."

"So, five new members?"

"Well, like I said, they're still testing."

As the sun moved across the sky, I moved to greet my new charges. Some didn't look at me, others glared at me, blame painfully evident in their eyes. I hugged them anyway. "Welcome. Let me know if you ever need anything."

When the sun went down and my people snuggled into bed, I crawled up into the Nest. To my surprise, the Senator soon joined me. "You're not on duty," I said in disbelief.

"Trace wasn't feelin' too well, so I said I'd take his shift." His grin, dim in the moonlight, sent a shiver of worry down my spine.

"What do you want, Robert?"

"Anala tells me you got scratched by that little girl."

My heart stopped. "Anala is a liar," I answered evenly, "and will do anything to discredit me."

"Oh, I see." Despite his tone of acceptance, I could tell he didn't believe me. Not that I expected him to. "Well, just for safety's sake, can I see your arm?"

Cold sweat beaded onto my skin. My nerves were suddenly on fire. I rolled my eyes, trying to appear annoyed. "I don't answer to you, and I don't answer to Anala."

"Then who do you answer to?"

"My people."

"Am I not one of your people? Isn't Anala?"

I didn't breathe. "You've both worked to undermine my authority. This is simply something you've concocted so my people will betray me."

"So bitter, Sammy." He shakes his head, clucking his tongue. "You know, every politician has his expiration date. What you've done is great for these people, but your time's up. You don't know anything about runnin' a large group of people."

"I'm not a politician," I spat. "I care for them. I feed them. I sacrifice for them. I make sure this camp runs smoothly."

"All behind that big galoot, Bubba. How powerful would you be without your guard dog by your side?"

I gritted my teeth. "It would make no difference. I've done right by them. They trust me. I don't want power over them. I want to save them."

"But you've made it quite clear that you don't trust them to make decisions for themselves." The conversational tone he was using to argue with me was infuriating. Just beneath the surface was a dark undercurrent, something knowing and threatening that made the hair on the back of my neck stand at attention. "You won't let them go outside the gates. You won't let them use currency to procure what they need. You make them abide by what you deem necessary for them to have. You kill them when they get sick."

"Thor was not safe!" I shouted. "I stand by my decision, Cuthridge. I've made decisions for this camp because someone has to. These are my people. They followed me first. This is the Eden I've created, and I won't have *you* coming in here making trouble where there is none just so you can reclaim whatever illusion of power you had as a Senator! If you don't like the way this place is run, I suggest you find your own camp, because this is mine, and as long as you reside here, you are subject to my laws." My face had contorted into a snarl, my voice low and lethal.

There was a long silence as we stared each other down. When he finally spoke, the courteous conversational tone was gone, replaced with something primitive and real, and I somehow found comfort in this dark side of the Senator. "Let me see your arm."

"No."

His eyes darkened, a triumphant grin splitting across his face like ice cracking on a lake. "What do you have to hide?"

"Nothing."

"Then why not show me your arm?"

"I owe you nothing, Cuthridge, and you owe me everything." I stepped closer to him, staring directly into his eyes, refusing to blink. "Watch yourself."

His smile did not fade. My stomach churned. The fear in my heart spread wings and escaped in the form of a shout for Bubba. The Senator laughed. "You see, Miss Sam, Anala's taken the precaution of making sure Bubba sleeps soundly through the night."

My heart sunk. For the first time since Brett's confession, I realized how powerless I was, even inside these walls. The only thing protecting me was social constructs. Outside of those, I could rely only on my own physical strength and brains. My muscles were wound tight, ready to spring. Every fiber of my being was vibrating. "What?"

"Little lady, we are staging a mutiny."

And something snapped inside of me. I lunged at him, knocking him to the floor of the Nest. He *howled*. I was only vaguely aware of my fists breaking against his face like waves during a hurricane.

"Shut up," I hissed. But it was too late. Below I could hear my people shuffling from their beds. I could hear the newborn screeching his displeasure at the jarring awakening.

In less than a minute, Beth was making her way up the ladder of the Crow's Nest. "What's going on?"

The Senator's fist smashed into my stomach, knocking the breath out of me. I doubled over in pain. He got to his feet quick as a flash. "Looks like your princess hasn't been one-hundred percent honest with y'all!" the Senator announced, his powerful voice resonating off of the walls. He grabbed my wrist and held my arm up to the light of Beth's flashlight, revealing the freshly scabbed over scratch. "She's been scratched by the Infected! Hasn't said a damn word to anyone!" He paused for dramatic effect. I jerked my arm out of his hand, hiding the scratch as if that could undo the damage. Below us sounded gasps of disbelief and outrage.

"She's lied to you about everything!" he continued. "She's been keeping you in poverty so that she can control you! She's imprisoned and threatened and brainwashed and even *killed* anyone who opposed her! And now here she is hiding the wounds she got from the very child she murdered!"

"No!" I shouted, but my voice wasn't as resonant. "I didn't murder her!"

"I saw you kill her!" someone shouted, but when I looked down I could only make out yellow orbs littering the sea of humanoid silhouettes.

"Don't listen to him! He's trying to poison you against me!"

"I'm trying to free you!" he shot back. "She's been keeping y'all in fear, telling you that you have to stay within these walls, telling you

you can't make a living, telling you that this infection is still a threat! This isn't a democracy! This is tyranny!"

A few shouts of agreement followed. I gaped, too shocked to respond. How dare my people betray me? My people...my followers. I had provided and cared for them and with just a few words they were swayed against me. I couldn't breathe.

"And now," the Senator continued in a softer voice, "she won't subject herself to the same laws she enforces. Ladies and gentlemen, this is not a leader—this is a Nazi."

"That's a lie!" I shrieked.

"Do you deny that you were scratched by one of the so-called Infected this morning?"

He was holding a trial in front of my people. He was kicking up enough rage and hatred so that when he turned them over to me, they would rip me to pieces.

"Do you deny that you killed anyone you deemed to be Infected?"

I couldn't speak.

"Do you deny that you've kept us in fear of the Infection to control the population?" He turned back to the crowd below. "When was the last time any of us saw an Infected? Is there *any* proof that the Infection is still around?"

"She lied to us!" another voice answered.

Bastards. Those ungrateful, scared bastards. I wanted to scream for Bubba. I wanted Brett. Why were none of my people offering to protect me?

"Scan her." It was Anala. "Scan her!"

My heart pounded so loudly I couldn't hear myself shout. "No! Those scans are faulty at best! Who knows how many false positives there have been?!" I covered my mouth when I realized what I had said.

An anguished cry echoed across the camp. "So you killed my daughter, knowing she might not have been Infected?"

My blood ran cold. I was terrified, and I was furious. I turned to the Senator. "Look what you've done!"

The Senator moved suddenly, and for the second time that day, I could barely piece together what happened. Something sharp jabbed up into my side, but it didn't hurt. "Go and face your people," the Senator sneered. His face was bright in the moonlight and for a moment I thought I saw Lucifer in his countenance. Suddenly I was grasping at thin air, my body hurtling toward the ground. Only when I heard the sickening crack of bones breaking did I realize that I'd been thrown from the Crow's Nest to the ground, and when I saw the bone jutting out of the skin of my arm, everything went dark.

The jarring pain of the stab wound and my broken arm brought me back to reality. I was shaking. I had vomited at some point. Anala stood before me, her gaze cold as ice.

"Anala, please, help me," I begged.

"We've not decided if you're to live or die, so we haven't wasted any resources on you." A dark smile split her lips. "I'm sure you're happy to hear that."

Fury surged through me as my words were misused. I moved to grab her neck but any movement was stopped by handcuffs. I was bound to the bed. "Anala," I growled, "how could you do this to me?"

"I'm just practicing what you preached, Sam."

I had never hated any of my people, but now I absolutely loathed Anala. I would have gladly marched through the gates of Hell if I could have handed her over to Satan himself. I would have traded my life for the opportunity to slice the skin from her bones.

Her unfeeling gaze stayed fixed on me as I writhed in pain.

At some point, I was given painkillers, just enough that I could stand during my trial. Funny that the Senator would toss me from the Crow's Nest and in less than three hours offer me a trial. Probably to save face. Would the Survivors follow a murderer?

Bubba pleaded on my behalf, reminding them of the systems I had implemented, reminding them that none of them had wanted for anything. Anala reminded them of Thor's death, how I'd ordered his execution while the others slept.

I was returned to the infirmary while the Camp decided my fate. They would vote, individually, and somehow I doubted that the Senator and Anala would play fair.

It was in the dark of that room that I turned my people over to the Senator. They were no longer mine. They had rejected me, and I could no longer protect them. They were no longer my responsibility. I mourned.

And then I raged.

I would destroy them.

This would end in flames.

∵   ∵   ∵

I built this camp up from the ashes. I knew areas that were rarely trodden; I knew which areas were stable. I knew where to hide from the watchmen at the Crow's Nest. While Anala slept, I slipped my wrists from the cuffs, biting on the blankets to quell my screams. I stabbed her with a scalpel. I don't know if she screamed, and I don't know how many times the blade penetrated her skin. I don't know if she was actually dead when I left her bleeding on her bed.

After raiding the supply closet for pain killers, I gathered the lighter fluid from the kitchen, and I barricaded the exit with firewood and debris. My rage far surpassed the pain. In fact, my body was buzzing with adrenaline.

While the Survivors slept, I set fire to Camp Phoenix using the Zippo I'd looted from the body of a small boy one year ago. I stood in the abandoned concrete street that led to the hospital, close enough that I could feel the heat that would snuff out the lives of the bastards that betrayed me, close enough that I could hear their screams. Anna Marie's. Max's. Daniel's.

I did not weep.

This is what happens you bite the hand that feeds. This is what happens when you betray your Goddess.

This is the Hell that I created.

About the Author

A fan of the "books and beer" culture, A. O'Neal moved to Asheville four years ago to work as a ministry assistant and hasn't looked back. She holds a bachelor of arts in Psychology and English from Mars Hill University. She is also the proud mum of sweet Labrador and a very grumpy hedgehog.

From Dark Alley Press; available wherever e-books are sold.

Nick, a London musician and bookstore manager, falls for a goth beauty he meets online. However, Suzy has a problem. No one believes a ghost is gradually taking over Suzy's life, until Nick and his friend Zac start to investigate. But is it too late for Suzy, who is gradually spiraling into a sordid decline?

Praise for The Tale of Storm Raven

"*The Tale of Storm Raven* is a hair-twisting, Koji Suzuki-style tale of the macabre that reminds us identity is fragile...fans of Japanese horror, don't miss this one!"

~ Kristi Petersen Schoonover, author of *Bad Apple*

From Dark Alley Press; available wherever print and e-books are sold.

From These Ashes chronicles the journey of two siblings looking for "home," while searching for themselves, each other, their heritage and their destiny. In a center for cult recovery in Phoenix, Arizona, 16-year-old Native American Naomi West refuses to talk; instead she writes—about her life, about her brother, about the prophecy, and about the fire that nearly destroyed it all. Meanwhile, her half-white brother, Tim West, awakes alone in a forest without memories of his past, only an unconscious urge to head west. It is on a Cascade mountaintop where he once again gets too close to a fire, and what starts as a horrifying nightmare wakens him to the truth of his past and a devastating choice that cost him everything.

From Vagabondage Press; available wherever print and e-books are sold.

Abe's story is one of either memory or madness; if only he could remember which. When Abe Finchley finally gets to meet the woman he has been looking for all his life, he finds not just beauty, but also love and family. It's a lifetime of dreams come true, but dream is just another word for nightmare and Abe knows all about those. Abe is going to have to make a difficult choice. It is a choice that might just destroy the world. *A Darker Moon* is a tale of the unlit places where it is best not to shine even the dimmest light.

Holly has been mortal all her life. Now at thirty-eight, her fairy godfather arrives to tell her she's a witch, and suddenly she's having to come to terms with the uncertainties of an alarmingly magic-fuelled world. Magic is not like it is in the books and films, and Holly starts to doubt whether her fairy godfather, Partridge Mayflower, is the fey, avuncular charmer he appears. When appearances are magically deceptive, Holly cannot afford to trust those closest to her, including herself.

AUTHORS WANTED FOR

INK STAINS ANTHOLOGIES

We are looking for unique dark fiction submissions for upcoming editions of *Ink Stains Anthology* from Dark Alley Press.

Submissions are now open for pieces 3,000-20,0000 words for all works that fit under the Dark Alley Press banner, including those in the following categories:

- Dark fiction (including lit fic)
- Gothic fiction
- Supernatural/paranormal fiction
- Horror
- Steampunk
- Black Comedy
- Fantasy and Sci Fi

Authors of acquired pieces for Ink Stains Anthology will receive a flat fee payment upon publication. For more information, check out the link below.

http://www.darkalleypress.com/inkstainsanthology